MAPMAKER'S MISTAKE

MEILANI SCHIJVENS

Published by Rain Coast Fables

Print Book ISBN: 978-0-578-81128-4

www.mapmakersmistake.com

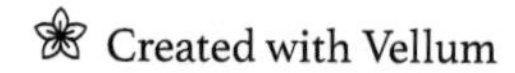

DEDICATION

Invented for my boys, Zayden and Denali, so I could "read" to them along Alaska's trails one summer, when they were younger.

Dedicated to Sig and Helen, forever riding through the wilds of Zanzia.

PROLOGUE

O*nce upon a time...*

"Is it a girl or a boy?" he asked the midwife. She held up the small bundle in her arms, a tiny face peering out.

"A girl, sir," she responded.

"Oh, thank God, thank God," the king replied, voice thick with relief. "We are saved. Now it all depends on her."

1

PRINCESS FOR SALE

Asha ducked as the arrow whizzed by, her horse snorting angrily beneath her. The green rolling hills of Zanzia lay in front of her, while the dark walls of the castle loomed behind.

"You almost hit me!" she yelled in the direction of the arrow. In response, Asha's attacker released another arrow, this time aimed at her head.

At thirteen, Asha was a beautiful girl. Her hair was golden and fell in loose ringlets. Right now, however, it was just in the way. She swiped at her hair furiously, annoyed it had fallen out of its braid, as she tried to get a better look at the arrow headed in her direction.

This time she used her sword as a bat, knocking the arrow out of the sky at the last possible second, both halves falling away. "And that was even closer!" she shouted.

Asha felt exposed. Her would-be assassin had made a nest in a nearby tree in the apple orchard and had the high ground. "The best defense is a good offense," she muttered to herself as she reeled her horse around, cantering directly toward the tree.

The lowest branches were too high up. Asha tucked her sword into the leather belt and stood on her horse. She leapt for the bottommost limb, legs swinging wildly, her horse riding on without her.

Asha knew her assailant well. It was her very own lady-in-waiting, the fourteen-year-old red-headed Rose. Asha climbed swiftly up the tree, through the branches thick with apples, using her sword to furiously strike at the leaves. She wore pants beneath her modified dress and split petticoat, allowing her to climb more easily than the ridiculous outfits princesses were traditionally required to wear.

"I'm coming for you Rose!" Asha taunted, as she climbed closer. A hard push up over a final branch, and she was face to face with her lady-in-waiting. Asha raised her sword to attack, just as Rose strung another arrow. For a moment they were at a standoff, staring one another down.

Sword versus arrow.

Suddenly a trumpet sounded, marking the beginning of the final trial and the end of this one.

"Looks like I won't be able to stay after all, your majesty," grinned Rose, as she climbed out to the end of a particularly large branch, which gracefully lowered her to the ground.

She jumped the final 10 feet, rolling as she absorbed the fall, immediately on her feet again, taking off at a full run. Asha tried to do the same, but the branch she selected broke halfway down.

Asha hit the ground hard, wind knocked out of her, landing painfully on the hilt of her sword. For a moment she just stared up at the mostly blue sky, taking mental inventory of her body, making sure she hadn't broken anything. Rose had gotten away, but Asha was not about to let her win that easily. Back on her feet, Asha placed two fingers in her mouth, whistling loudly before she took off running after Rose.

Asha saw Rose looking back, grinning, the finish line just over the rise. Asha willed herself to run faster. She was making gains on Rose, but it would not be enough.

Just then Asha's horse erupted beside her in full canter. She swung up into the saddle in a fluid motion. With a burst of speed, she flew past Rose.

The assembled crowd of villagers in tattered clothes cheered as Asha made it past the finish line first, collapsing on the ground as her friend reached her moments later.

"It's not fair your horse comes when you whistle! Mine just ignores me," Rose protested, falling onto Asha in a heap on the ground. "I was so sure I had you that time! Also, I'm not sure I can get up anymore. I'm just going to lie here for a while." Rose added, with a twinkle in her eye, "And what were you going to do anyways, stab me with your wooden sword?"

"It would have served your right for nearly hitting me with your arrows!" Asha remonstrated.

"Cork arrows," Rose emphasized. "They would have barely hurt you at all. I can't believe Max won't let us use real weapons. You should be very impressed that I can come that close to hitting anything with those silly, awkward arrows, let alone a pesky princess on a horse who insists on constantly moving! I should get an award for that I think." She repositioned to use Asha's stomach as a pillow.

Asha playfully pushed Rose off of her. "First one to the stables wins!"

"Oooh, I hate you, your majesty!" said Rose, already running to catch up.

"Yes, everybody hates me, that's why they are selling me!" Asha shouted back over her shoulder.

"Thank goodness for that," teased Rose. She didn't mean it, of course. Asha was her favorite person in the world.

Asha was only six when she discovered the dark secret of her kingdom of Zanzia. In order for Zanzia to survive, it was going to require one, tiny, sacrifice: Asha herself.

Six-year-old Asha had beat her older cousin at chess three times in a row, before he exploded.

"You know what? I'm glad your parents are selling you off. I wish they had gotten rid of you already!" he had yelled, tipping over the board in anger, the black king and white pawns shattering on the cold marble floor as he stomped out, leaving the chamber silent.

This was, of course, news to Asha, but she was also certain that it wasn't true. Asha was the eldest daughter of the Zanzia Royal Family, and as the eldest princess she was heir to the throne. She was not worried, but she ran off to find her mother anyhow, mostly frustrated by her cousin's lack of sportsmanship and wanting to find a reassuring lap to sit upon.

And so that is how the deeply guarded secret no one was ever to tell the princess – at least not until she was significantly older – was revealed. Her mother, the queen, could only reassure her it wasn't *exactly* true, and that her cousin really *shouldn't* have said it. There would be no comforting lap. And for Asha, as she came to understand, there would be no Zanzian throne.

2

A MAPMAKER'S MISTAKE

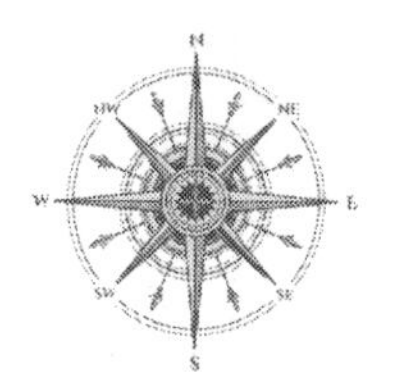

Asha had barred herself in her room, only relenting to open the door to her beloved servant Orrin. Orrin was a doddering old man, even when Asha was little. She loved his kind eyes and white bushy eyebrows fiercely. And so it fell to Orrin to tell her the whole tale. The very sad story of Zanzia and her nation's desperate trade standing in the world due to problematic relations with Zanzia's neighbors to the north.

"It has been such a fine land you see." Orrin began. Asha crawled into his lap, like she was a kitten, listening to the story that would determine her entire life. Orrin continued.

"The kingdom of Zanzia had once been large and prosperous. It was a fertile valley that stretched to the coastal trading routes with a healthy, happy populace that farmed lands and herded cows, using these crops for trade throughout the kingdoms.

One day a funny thing happened, but not something that would seem to have any bearing on Zanzia's status as a thriving nation. An apprentice mapmaker in the northern kingdom of Nadroj accidentally created a map showing Zanzia's coastal areas belonging to Nadroj, and that map was mistakenly submitted in the place of his master's. The king of Nadroj and the Queen of Zanzia at the time laughed at it over tea and tea cakes.

"How preposterous!" the king of Nadroj had said. The kingdom of Nadroj was hundreds of miles to the north and didn't even connect to the coast. "Just what are they teaching at mapmaking schools these days, anyhow?"

The official maps were to be corrected immediately, just as soon as the king arrived back home.

Unfortunately for the Zanzians, the king never arrived home. A freak accident with a horse left the king thrown off with a broken neck, and he died before ever setting foot in his beloved Nadroj again. And as is the way with families and kingdoms from time to time, his crown was passed along to his oldest son, who despite occasional flashes of brilliance was haunted by demons that no one but he could see. The young king screamed at nothing and at everyone, and would, at times, walk around entirely naked, muttering that his clothes were laced with rat poison. Rules of succession as they were, the Nadroj people could do nothing.

The young king's royal advisors did the only thing they could, marrying him off to an ill-fated woman of appropriate social standing. Their goal was to wait it out until the next heir could be procured by the royal pairing. The miserable new young queen soon became pregnant.

It could not have been a happy childhood for the young Dokar, the product of that union. Upon his birth his mother handed off the infant to the royal advisors as quickly as she could, and left in the night, never to return. The royal advisors of Nadroj secured the best tutors for young Dokar, dressed him in the finest robes, and taught him the art of diplomacy and sword play – while his father railed against false demons and succumbed to paranoia."

"He must have been a very sad and lonely boy," said Asha, speaking up for the first time.

"I believe he was. That poor child, I believe he was," said Orrin as he continued, stroking her hair tenderly.

"It was against this backdrop that the Zanzia kingdom tried to get the map changed back. But getting the attention of the king was impossible, and the advisors used his rare moments of lucidity to address more pressing domestic matters. And so, when Prince Dokar became King Dokar he could rightly point out that the "border dispute" (as he called it) had been going on for nearly 20 years and throughout the reigns of three kings. He had no intention of relinquishing Nadroj's coastal property. Zanzia appealed to its other neighbors, only to fully and for the first time understand what sort of king Dokar would be.

The assemblage of leaders came to Nadroj to congratulate Dokar on ascending to the throne. Once the matter of the coastal lands was raised Dokar stated that he saw the entire kingdom of Zanzia as an enemy nation on a quest to steal Nadroj land, and any nation trading with Zanzia would be seen as declaring an act of war. Retribution, King Dokar warned, would be swift and deadly.

The Zanzians loved their bustling port cities, the fresh seafood that filled their marketplaces, and the picnics and holidays on the sandy beaches. While the error of the map had been theoretically maintained during this entire period, its effect had never been felt. Now, seemingly overnight, the prosperous days of the Zanzian kingdom had ended. Dokar's seemingly endless supply of professional soldiers forcefully occupied the coastal zone marked on the false map. Zanzia had no real army, just a collection of armed farmers and fishermen who could not hold the seashore towns. Zanzia found itself with no allies to lend aid because crossing Dokar meant attracting his wrath as well.

Trading ended, and Zanzia became landlocked and alone. All the fishermen and seafarers, whose boats were not yet commandeered by Dokar's men, sailed to new lands where they could live safely. Zanzia, a coastal country without a sea, slowly began to suffocate.

Dokar's army then descended on Zanzia's northern territory. Overnight the army moved the border a couple hundred yards. The next night, a couple hundred more. Slowly Zanzia's northern lands shrank by miles. With no army to muster, Zanzia sent farmers to the north to defend the border and ensure it didn't move in the darkness. But thousands of farmers not farming meant that the northern border was secure at the expense of diminished food supplies. Women and children took the men's place in the fields. Schools emptied out and education happened intermittently. Cloth was something that could no longer be brought in through the borders, so Zanzians made fabric themselves and clothing became rough and basic.

The great thinkers of Zanzia tried to come up with a solution. Anything that would improve their hopeless fate. Try as they did, they could only come up with one desperate idea that could possibly fix everything.

What they needed was a girl, a baby girl, the heir to the throne. For if you marry off a female heir to another kingdom, you get a queen's dower in return – a huge gift of power transferred from one kingdom to another. And with the right pairing, and with the right kingdom, that gift could just be big enough to save Zanzia.

A girl for a kingdom."

"You mean me," said Asha sadly, hollowly. "All because somebody didn't pay attention to their lessons and made a bad map. And because there was a sad boy who grew up to be a mean king."

"Well," said Orrin gently, "You hadn't even been born yet. So it wasn't you when they came up with the idea. It wasn't personal. But I'm so sorry my sweet girl. It turned out to be you. You are a very special girl, you see. People are hoping that when you grow up, you can save us all."

"How grown up?" asked Asha.

This time Orrin didn't answer, because in truth, he didn't know, and he was also not sure how long Zanzia could survive before they needed Asha to be that girl that would save them.

Asha was born to be that girl. The girl who was to be given away, traded, sold, so that every other person in her kingdom could live.

When Asha had finally emerged during breakfast the next day she was famished and furious. She no longer looked like a six-year-old princess but a fierce tomcat. She had sliced up her clothing with a tiny penknife to remove all ruffles and bows, so only the practical bits remained. She had also cut off her hair. Her long princess tresses, that she had been so admired for, had been shorn with the same small blade. A heap of golden ringlets lay discarded on her floor.

She burst into the cold dining room where King Henrick and Queen Kirsten were having their oatmeal and coffee. "It isn't very nice that you are going to sell me. I don't like it at all!" Asha glowered at them all, as if she was the only adult there, and her parents needed a talking to.

Both the king and queen protested at once.

"We are not *selling* you. You know princesses sometimes have to get married for their kingdoms. This is like that," her mother tried to say in soothing tones.

"We are only trying to do what is best for our kingdom and for you," said her father.

But Asha was having none of it.

"I want to stay in Zanzia. If I can fight that mean king, I will win! Teach me how to sword fight. And ride horses. And if I can't beat him, only then you can sell me. But I get to try first. You have to let me try!" Her teacup voice had taken on a new edge and volume.

The queen sighed. She had no other idea or plan to save the kingdom – except to marry off her little girl once she became of age. Kirsten and Henrick exchanged an almost imperceptible nod of agreement.

"And one more thing." said Asha.

"What is it?" asked the queen gently.

"Please, please don't make me get married when I'm 10 or 13. Only when I'm older, like 18, right?" asked Asha, plaintively.

King Henrick knew in his heart that the kingdom couldn't last another twelve years. But that would be a conversation for another day. For now, what other choice did they have, really, then to agree to Asha's terms.

Trousers and riding boots appeared in her closet that evening. The very next morning, after a breakfast of curds and whey, she was led out to the courtyard, which was mostly being used for the storage of hay, given a miniature wooden sword, and her very own soldier to train her.

3

QUEST FOR A FRIEND

Little Asha had taken to her training with a gusto only seen in the fiercest of warriors. She was tireless in her exercises, putting all of her rage and disappointment into every swing of her miniature sword. She would arise before dawn, already battling the wet burlap sacks of hay that had been hung in the courtyard for her. Her trainer, Ben, would find her there, soaked by the morning's rain, tiny face scrunched red in exertion, while the heavy bags swayed harmlessly against the onslaught of the little girl. Ben wasn't exactly a soldier. He was a teenager who had served on the northern front when his turn had come up, he was good with his younger siblings, and his family's farm could spare him for that season.

The Queen drank coffee and watched her daughter with deep sorrow and a heavy heart. "At least we must find her a companion," the Queen said to her husband. "Asha's path is dark and lonely. We must ensure that she does not have to walk it alone. She needs a friend."

"She has her sister," said the King. "And she has us. We are enough."

"Aurelia is but a baby. She is not yet a friend. And with Asha to be married off and losing her right as oldest to take the throne, that honor will fall on her sister. She is going to need someone to help guide her through the rich trials that will be her life. She needs someone besides her sister, and besides the parents who bestowed this fate upon her."

Messengers were deployed, and soon their requests were met with success in the Kingdom of Pome, a seaside country that was less than a week away by horseback. The Queen of Pome had a lady-in-waiting with three daughters, who had lost her husband. The first two were noble little ladies, who fit in beautifully with the Pome palace life, loved their pretty dresses, and perfecting their curtseys. These two would surely follow in their mother's footsteps.

The third was an unruly seven-year-old cub, who was constantly reprimanded for taking shortcuts across palace roofs, escaping her duties by absconding to the royal stables to talk to the horses, and showing up with muddied dresses to her etiquette lessons. Her mother had named her Rose, with the misplaced idea that she would blossom like her sisters. But Rose was all thorns. Her wild red hair was always wild, and the hems of her dresses were always getting snagged and torn.

In other words, she was perfect for Asha.

Rose's mother, Lady Marza, asked if she wanted to give up the cultured life of Pome. "Rose, you have been offered an opportunity in Zanzia. You would have to move to Zanzia to be the lady-in-waiting to their princess, Meliasha DeBurn. She is six and you will be expected to play outside with her, probably get dirty, ride horses, and practice sword fighting. Are you interested?"

"Mama," replied Rose with a sigh. "I already know this is a trick question! If I say yes of course, you are going to give me yet another of your lectures on the importance of being a proper lady. Which I just don't want to hear again right now, and so I should say no."

"Daughter," said Lady Marza sternly. "This is indeed a serious offer. You have been handpicked by a queen as the best-suited child in many kingdoms around to fulfill this role. It is yours, should you want it."

"In that case I want to go! Thank you, mama, thank you!" yelped Rose, jumping up and down with excitement, hugging Lady Marza, and dancing around the room.

At almost eight years old, Rose had seen the long, dull world of her indoor frilly life unfold before her eyes, and she had been dreading every moment of it. Giving up her sisters would be easy – they'd never really bonded. Well, they had bonded with each other, but never her. Saying goodbye to her mother was the only hard part of her choice.

Rose arrived several weeks later on horseback, smuggled in the darkest hour of the night to avoid the Nadroj sentries that forbid trade in and out of Zanzia. But Rose didn't mind. For once in her life, she was having a proper adventure. She imagined she was a pirate captain trying to elude capture.

Rose arrived at Zanzia just before dawn on a Tuesday. Asha was already at work, hacking angrily and with little effect at burlap sacks, as pink and golden clouds lit up the vast green fields. Rose jumped off the back of the horse she'd been riding with a smile so broad and contagious that the little princess found it impossible to maintain her perfected rage.

"Hi! I'm Rose. And you must be Meliasha DeBurn. Is there a sword around here for me too?" Rose said brightly.

"I'm just Asha, and my whole kingdom is going to crumble. Unless they make me marry someone I don't want to." Asha replied. "You can use that sword over there. But be careful of the splinters."

Rose was the perfect sparring companion for little Asha. The two made up endless fighting games and set up complicated competitions that involved horse jumping, sword fighting, archery, and always ended with a breathless foot race.

These became weekly events, and soon drew a crowd of spectators. At first it was just the children of Zanzia who came to watch, but soon everyone wanted to see the two fierce little girls in battle with each other. At first Rose won easily, being the bigger of the two. But as the months and years crept by, Asha caught up, being the more competitive and aggressive of the pair.

No matter the outcome, Rose ended each race in a heap of laughter and a delighted twinkle in her eye. Asha, however, would instead think about how she could improve, and how she would go harder and faster the next time. Little Aurelia would always be on the sidelines, watching the older girls, her own miniature bow and arrow on her back, a pair of brown braids down her back, cheering the loudest of anyone.

Rose gave them all a sense of levity and joy. Too long had the kingdom been shrouded in the mists of despair. To see Rose experience their bleak world as a paradise beyond measure gave them all more resolve, and a little bounce to their step.

But it was not all war games and horseback riding. The girls were also expected to be educated in the manner befitting an heir the crown. Math, history, astronomy, philosophy, literature, and the dreaded etiquette curriculum. For these last classes, they had to put on their forgotten, cast off dresses, drink tea with their pinkies facing the correct way, and practice niceties, which the girls would do with far too much enunciation, and which left them both in a fit of giggles that certainly was not befitting of ladies of their standing. But in spite of themselves they excelled at all of it, from marksmanship to chess to the harp.

Even as the world around them continued to crumble and decline.

4

SWORD MASTER

"Again Asha! Again!" called out their instructor Max, on yet another misty early morning drill. It was the morning after the competition in which Asha had beat Rose in the apple orchard. For years he had been tutoring Asha and Rose on the art of swordsmanship.

Max had come into their lives five years earlier.

When Asha was eight, a ragged man and woman appeared at the Northern border. That they had walked over the mountains from Nadroj, avoiding soldiers in the middle of the coldest, darkest part of the winter would have been remarkable in its own right; but the man arrived with a gaping wound, recently having been separated from his left hand.

So few strangers turned up in Zanzia these days that despite their condition, they were treated to a generous welcome of coffee and blankets, medical attention and an empty hut to stay in. The man, it turned out, was none other than the great Nadroji swordsman Max Brintmore, who had been the sparring instructor to Dokar, the despotic Nadroji king. Max told the Zanzians that took him in that he had been proud to have been asked to train the king in swordsmanship. His father had been the sword master to Dokar's kindly grandfather, and he considered it a great honor to uphold the family tradition.

And then he told the story of how he lost his hand.

Max had begun training the king just over a year ago. It took a year of sparring and each time Max bested the king, understanding that it was his duty to help Dokar find his weaknesses and improve them. After a year, Dokar finally found an opening in Max's onslaught, and, in a move Max had taught him, wretched the sword away from his master. Max's first instinct was pride. But before the teacher could congratulate his pupil, or even pick up his sword, and say, let's-try-that-again, the king did something Max had not anticipated.

Dokar screamed, elated in his victory, "I am better than you. I beat you, old man. I don't need that hand anymore, which means you don't need it either!"

In a swift move Dokar decapitated Max's hand from his arm. Max writhed on the ground in agony, but the king just laughed, spit on him, and kicked at him where he lay. Max crept home to the cottage he shared with his wife, Martha, and they immediately embarked on the treacherous journey over the mountains. Max and Martha knew that the king was not a generous man or one who displayed penance or remorse. It was more likely that the king would return the next day for an encore than amends, and neither of them wanted to be there for a second act.

Asha, hearing all of this from Orrin, immediately asked her father for an audience with Max.

Asha, how do we know this is not a trick?" Her father demanded, clearly being against the meeting. "How can we trust him? He is a Nadroji army commander. From the day you were born we have kept your identity a secret. Dokar knows what you being a girl would mean to us. We cannot risk this."

"Father, that's just silly," Asha said in her most reasonable voice, "His hand really **is** missing, and nobody, let alone a sword fighter, would ever go to such lengths on purpose just to trick us. And he is the only one who can really teach me how to beat Dokar in a sword fight. Let me train with Dokar's sword master. Please daddy?" Asha pleaded, and because King Henrick could never say no to his daughter, the meeting was granted.

Max was sitting on the floor of the hut he had been given to live in. It was a small but tidy abode, with cushions on the floor. Asha came in and quietly sat across from the much older man, her eyes wide with trepidation and hope, studying his wrinkles and a scar that ran across his forehead.

Max eyed the princess with bemusement. "But you are a girl? How can this be! There is no one who suspects you are indeed not a prince. This is a surprise!"

"Well," said Asha very seriously, "Will you betray us, now that you know my secret?" Max laughed, a deep, kind but soft chuckle.

"Oh, my little princess, would I betray you to Dokar? To the man who severed my hand as gratitude for my teachings? I would not. And just to prove it, I will tell you my own secret, which is also the reason that I fled." Asha decided that she liked this older man immediately and settled into the cushions of the room to listen to his deep, rich baritone voice.

"You see I fought and trained Dokar everyday – fighting him with this now missing hand." He held up his left arm to make the point, but his eyes twinkled mischievously. "I was trying to encourage him but not best him too easily. I hadn't intended it to be a secret. That day was supposed to be his graduation day to the next level. Instead he believed I had nothing left to teach him." Asha leaned in, interested but confused. Max continued. "I knew if he knew my secret, his embarrassment over his treatment of me could not be remedied. And so, I took my wife and we ran. It took two weeks to cross the mountains without a horse, but it was that or guaranteed death. You see, mine was not a closely guarded secret."

"But I don't see," Asha remarked. "What is your secret?"

Max held up his injured arm again. "I, my child, am not left-handed." Max held up his unharmed right arm with a smirk of triumph and wiggled his fingers. Asha and the old man laughed. They laughed until they cried, and tears ran from their eyes. The very next day Asha's real training began.

"Asha! Focus! Try it again." called out Max, pulling Asha back into the present.

These days Asha trained with Max as if a battle between her and Dokar could happen any day. In truth, the reality of it happening was far-fetched at best. King Dokar seemed content to sit idly upon his throne and chip away at Zanzia one square foot of land at a time rather than present himself personally. And if he did come, it would hardly be Asha who would fight him. She was simply too valuable to ever be allowed to get near him. She was worth more to Zanzia than anyone else in the kingdom. She would be protected and coddled from any such fight ever occurring. But the effort she put forth in her training seemed to give Asha a sense of control over her fate, and so the king allowed the training to continue. And so, she continued to train.

The particular technique she was working on with Max was difficult, and everything depended on the timing. The enemy king, Dokar, apparently took great pleasure in starting a sword fight with his weaker hand (oh the irony, thought Asha). At some point during the fight (especially if he was winning) Dokar would make a dramatic comment about being finally ready to start fighting in earnest and toss his sword up with a twirl before he caught it with his other hand. It was a ridiculous gesture with an exploitable weakness.

Max was confident that Asha's abilities might one day exceed that of his former pupil, but he also wanted to make sure she would be able to take advantage of this easier way to win. So, they kept at it. Max would suddenly toss up his sword, giving the hilt a spin for good measure, and catch it again (in the same hand, of course, since he had only one.) Her task was to leap up and catch the guard loop with the tip of her own sword, and then catch her opponent's sword with her free hand.

She could do it every time with Rose, but Max was taller, putting the tossed twirling sword out of reach. And so, she had to jump, catch the sword handle with the tip of her sword, and try not to severely injure either of them before she could redirect the stolen sword into her open hand. Occasionally she did manage it, but Max would not give her a chance to celebrate or pause before immediately making her attempt it again.

And that was exactly how Asha wanted it.

5

NORTHERN FRONT

The next morning Asha and Rose set out to the northern border to pay a visit to the troops.

For so many years now, farmers continued to take their turn at the border, pretending to be soldiers. It was excruciatingly boring and lonely work. Farmers would leave their farms and families with endless chores needing to be done, cows that needed to be milked, land that needed to be hoed, crops that needed to be planted or brought in, fences that needed fixing, roofs that needed thatching ... the lists were never-ending. They would present themselves at the northern border for three-month tours of duty and sit futilely by, waiting for something to happen. The border was long, and it took a tremendous number of men to secure it, each serving long shifts by themselves in complete idleness.

The girls were the best suited to cheer the troops up. Every time they came, saddle bags laden with special provisions, the men would see that Asha was growing up. Their main job, as they saw it, was to sit wantonly by the border until she was old enough to save the kingdom. Every time they saw her growing incrementally older, it was a sign that their job as caretakers was closer to being done.

No one knew exactly how she was actually supposed to go about saving the kingdom. What were the mechanics of it? She would marry some prince, and that prince would come from a powerful kingdom and they would send...what. Soldiers? Weapons? Gold? They would have greater negotiation power with the Nadroji? To make a new map? A peace and trading treaty? Each outcome seemed as wildly unlikely as the last. Why would anyone come all the way to Zanzia to save some impoverished farmers? It didn't make a whole lot of sense to anyone. There appeared to be no actual plan, just a potential end date, after which Asha would be ceremoniously handed over to the highest bidder, a great gift would be bestowed to their kingdom in exchange, and everything would magically be okay.

But believing in happily ever after magic, when you have nothing else left to believe in can be powerful for morale, and no one wanted to collapse that fragile bubble of hope. And so, they repeated to themselves, over their never-ending shifts, the date of Asha's 18th birthday like a mantra, like a prayer.

The girls would have preferred to ride bareback, but supplies were needed, and so they outfitted the horses and themselves for the long ride. It was three full days of riding to the front, with almost nothing in between – no towns, no building, hardly any homes. There was a remote inn where they could stay on the first night and more properly rest the horses, but the rest of the time it was just them and the wilds of Zanzia. Asha and Rose loved these days. Just the two of them, their horses, the wind, the wildflowers in endless fields, and forest groves. They dressed as boys in the thick coarse materials of the Zanzians, not for the sake of disguise, but because they couldn't ride very far in ladies' skirts, or really hardly at all.

They held mock battles as they rode. Rose would shoot arrows at Asha (real ones) and Asha would sweep them away with her sword. This was not safe play by any means. They raced to distant landmarks ("race you to the top of the hill!" "race you to the big tree!"), and dared each other to do foolish things ("how long can you ride standing up? I bet I can beat you!") Their faux skirmishes were endless and delightful.

On the second night, Asha and Rose built a campfire and set up to sleep out under the stars. They played chess under the moon – the night sky bright with stars and galaxies.

"I loved every minute of today," Asha said, moving her knight. "Right now, I feel like all of Zanzia is mine. I love all of this so much," she said, gesturing to the rolling hills, and the silhouette of a rugged mountain range against the darkening sky. "I don't ever want to have to leave."

"Oh, don't think about that yet." said Rose, moving out of check. "We have many more years of Zanzian days just like this one."

"But is Zanzia going to make it five more years until I'm 18 Rose?" asked Asha, moving her queen forward. "Our troops look more ragged every time we head to the north. The border keeps slipping further. The Nadroj army just waits around to take full advantage of any openings to creep the border forward during the times any part of it is unattended."

"At least no fighting ever takes place," said Rose kindly. "I mean, I love our Zanzian army, but they are hopelessly out matched to put it mildly.

"Yes," said Asha, "but I don't know how much longer our kingdom will hold. I know I'm being selfish. I don't think I can count on five more years of freedom. And every other week my mother tells me the name of some new prince, who turns out to be nearly 70 and the size of an elephant...but otherwise a truly fantastic catch." Rose giggled at this.

"We can't even count on tomorrow. Who knows what the future will hold? I don't!" Rose said, pressing forward with her queen again. "A silly student-mapmaker blew up your entire life before you were even born because he forgot where some squiggly lines were supposed to be, and so here we are. And someday, probably when you get married, I am going to be sent back to Pome to become a proper lady. But I am not going to spend anytime dwelling on that. Instead I am just going to enjoy days like today when we have them."

"Oh, don't be ridiculous Rose, you could never go back to Pome now, you could never manage the curtsies and the frills – and lack of things to shoot," said Asha teasing her friend. "I will leave you in charge of something important and you at least can stay in Zanzia forever. You will become Zanzia's Minister of Arrows." Asha laughed and then shouted into the night sky, "To Rose the Minister of Arrows!"

"I would be a most excellent Minister of Arrows," said Rose, delighted, despite knowing that there was no such thing. The girls talked deep into the night and fell asleep to the sounds of the Zanzian nighttime wilderness.

The next day they changed into dresses of their own design. At least they appeared to be dresses but were really pants camouflaged by layers of split skirts so that they could more easily mount and ride their horses. After so many years of training in decorum, they understood the importance of being *perceived* as being proper and regal, even when it felt like farce and illusion. Their dresses contained sheaths of silk that flowed behind them majestically, completing the spectacle. Rose's dress looked quite dramatic with her long red wild locks. She never could keep her hair as tame as Asha's, but of course she also had much less inclination to do so. Her goal was merely to contribute to the vision of Asha's regality. Just before they arrived, Asha added the last detail – her simple but elegant crown.

Once properly outfitted, Asha and Rose brought their steeds over the final hill on their way to the border.

The first moments of arrival were a bit like Christmas. Asha and Rose reached the camp and dismounted, presents in hand, and the men that were at the camp swarmed around them, slightly star struck to have the two girls in their midst.

Asha worried about the men. Each time they were showing more signs of wear and decline. Their "weapons" were just modified farming tools, scythes and shovels and the occasional old rusty sword. Their clothing and boots were faded and ragged, and their faces were gaunt. They looked less like the cavalry and more like prisoners of war. At least Asha had one immediate solution. Out of the girl's saddle bags came jerky (but the good kind), fresh cheese, eggs, and chocolate. The men cheered and broke out in a scattered applause. This was celebratory and lovely and expected.

But what happened in the next moment would change everything.

6

ATTACK

Suddenly, from the other side of the border and up a hill came a swarm of hundreds of horses and their riders. Unlike the nonexistent uniforms of the farmer army, these men were clad in crisp buttoned crimson jackets (brass gleaming in the sun), matching caps, and more alarming, real weapons. The troops descending down the hill had actual swords that looked shiny and sharp. There was a collective gasp from among the farmers as time slowed in the horror of it all.

Without thinking or pausing Asha leaped up onto her steed, unsheathed her sword, and galloped in the direction of the onslaught.

"HALT! she screamed at the incoming stampede, raising her sword into the air.

There was a peculiar amphitheater acoustic element in that particular spot in the mountains, and she managed to hit the spot perfectly as she cried out. Whether it was that, or the even more peculiar sight of a striking young teenager in a silk dress with her hair streaming out behind her on a war horse with a crown and a sword in hand coming directly at them, the men on horses obeyed. They stopped directly in front her. These were men who were used to following orders.

For a moment a strange silence hung in the air, as they all just stopped and gaped at each other. A formidable army versus one small girl.

From the back of the pack a voice broke through, “Why are you stopping, I didn’t tell you to stop!” Without ever having seen him Asha knew at once exactly who this voice belonged to. She sheathed her sword, hands trembling, and took a deep breath to steady her screaming nerves. Here was her mortal enemy. She had to think. She would only get one shot at this.

She raised her voice again; confident she was still in the correct spot to be heard above the din. “Your majesty! Good King Dokar! We did not know we were to have the pleasure of a formal state visit from our Northern neighbors today. Welcome to Zanzia!”

Rose appeared from behind Asha’s left side, arrow cocked in her bow just in case. Rose, her red hair and blue dress, struck quite the vision next to Asha.

King Dokar awkwardly pushed his horse through the stalled throng of horses to move to the front of the fray. "And who are you?!" he called out when he finally arrived. Asha was quietly amused that his location did not have the same acoustic qualities, and his words came out thin and reedy in contrast to her own. It was the first time Asha had gotten a look at this man she had imagined so many times. He had greasy ash blond hair, greying near his temples. His face was slightly pockmarked, perhaps the remains of a childhood illness. He was heavier than Asha had imagined.

Once again she raised her voice. "I am crown princess Meliasha Esmerelda DeBurn of the Zanzia! These are my men," she gestured to the meager group behind her. "This is our land! Today it seems that I am your gracious host, and you are my guest! It is my pleasure to finally meet you! I have heard great things about your majesty!"

"And I have heard nothing about you!" Dokar sputtered disdainfully. "A crown princess? Preposterous! I would have been told!"

"And yet, here I am! To what do I owe the pleasure of your visit today, your highness?" She worked to keep the rage and tremble out of her voice. She tried to sound strong and regal. In truth she was terrified.

"It is not a friendly visit, child. I have come to finally see this ridiculous Zanzian border myself."

"Ridiculous your majesty? You are in the magnificent country of Zanzia. But now that you have seen it, you are welcome to move along. *Your highness.*" She said these last two words more contemptuously then she meant to, and worked to make her face look sweet, in contrast.

"If you are indeed the crown princess, then you know there has been a game of cat and mouse along this border for far too long." Dokar spat at the ground. "I am here with my army to finally speed things along. In fact, it works out well that you are present. You will get to witness the end of your magnificent Zanzia." He narrowed his cold eyes at her. "In a moment I am going to have my men attack your men, and may the best army win." Dokar gave Asha a slightly sickening victorious smile.

Asha felt the bile rise up in the back of her throat. This wouldn't be a battle; it would be annihilation, she thought to herself. Her men would be massacred. A battle now, here, would mean the end of the war, the end of Zanzia, the end of everything.

She had only one idea. One last bubble of hope.

Asha smiled, innocently and serene. "King Dokar, I think I have a better idea," she interjected, "if you are amenable to hearing it."

Before he could object, she continued. "It is true that your army could fight my army. But you can see as well as I that my army is an honorable group of men who just want to get back to their farms. Now maybe they could beat your men, and maybe they could not, but I would hate to see any of them injured or killed, and unable to return to their fields.

We don't need a large, messy battle today. Couldn't we just settle this one-on-one?" She cocked her head slightly and continued smiling sweetly.

King Dokar looked at her, mouth slightly agape. But something seemed to click, and his eyes looked cold and pleased. "Fine, let's get on with it then. Major Hammond!" He gestured to a large brute of a man barely contained by his shiny brass buttons. Each button seemed ready to shoot off on its own accord and seriously injure someone. The Major grunted in reply.

"Oh no, you mistake my meaning your highness," Asha continued in her overly sweet and girly tone. "I thought it best for our leader to have a duel with your leader. I was proposing a match between myself and you, King Dokar!"

Shocked murmuring could be heard from among King Dokar's army.

They must think me very foolish and naïve, thought Asha. She dismounted her steed. She was the smallest person in the entire assemblage, and standing on the battlefield in her flowy dress, next to her large warhorse, she looked very tiny indeed.

King Dokar, who seemed to have been caught on his back foot during the exchange up until this point, suddenly was on more solid footing. "You and I? You are but a child. You and I will fight and settle the border dispute right here and now? Is that your plan? Fine. Then I am agreed!" Dokar said with a cold chuckle. To the men gathered near him he quietly added, "It looks like this is going to be over even more quickly and easily than we thought."

Asha madly tried to remember all of her art of negotiation lessons. The fate of her entire nation depended on her getting this next part exactly right.

"Thank you for your agreement your majesty. Of course, before we begin, we must decide on the terms of the exchange, and properly document our arrangement."

"Terms!" sputtered King Dokar. "The discussion of terms is going to be longer than the event itself. Why even bother? But fine, let's get on with it."

After some back and forth, what was agreed to was this. The fight would not be to the death, but to first blood, or if one's weapon was lost. It would be a sword fight. (Dokar seemed particularly pleased about this aspect, appearing to think he had outsmarted her.)

The location of the fight was to be very close to where they were standing. Asha had chosen a location where her voice could be heard among the assembled, and there was a perfectly sized rock. Dokar couldn't care less about the location of the duel, but Asha had a plan that included the rock. It was key to her strategy.

Now that Dokar saw there was a crown princess instead of a crown prince, he immediately understood the larger implications, just as the queen had always feared. King Dokar was not a fool. If he won, under the terms agreed, Asha would return with him to Nadroj to become his wife. And as a sign of his generosity, King Dokar promised to forego the border fight entirely. He correctly believed that the key to owning the entire kingdom of Zanzia lay in this royalette, and not in an arbitrary border location.

Asha readily agreed to all of it, never losing her childlike smile that hid a barrage of emotions underneath. "And if I win," Asha stated, "you will depart my lands at once. On foot. My men will keep your horses, your swords, and your jackets." She turned back to glance upon her pauper's army and smiled. "And the hats."

This last comment about the hats, or berets to be precise, drew snickering from the Nadroj soldiers, and even from some Zanzian ones.

"And," continued Asha, "you will promise not to invade my country for a period of at least ten years. And ..." she took a deep breath, "you will honor the borders of the original map of King Nret, your grandfather! Once again Zanzia's borders will reach the ocean and our trade with other nations will resume without interference!"

The Zanzian men started to cheer, but she silenced them with a fierce look and a gesture with her hand.

Asha was stunned by her own words. She worried she had gone too far, been too brash. But King Dokar appeared delighted by her demands, clearly loftily confident in his imminent success. He looked like a fox that had a mouse by its tail, dangling from its mouth.

“Have you a scribe?” she said, “Or shall I have my lady-in-waiting write down these terms?”

King Dokar had indeed not thought to bring a scribe to an ambush, so Rose wrote up the agreement.

Rose wrote slowly and carefully, both to make sure she had it all exactly right and to give Asha time to prepare. Rose willed her hand not to tremble as she wrote the terms that could perhaps change Zanzia’s future. Her eyes avoided Asha. In Asha’s princess costume, complete with crown and frilly purple, pastel silks, she looked too vulnerable and small to compete against this horrible man. King Dokar had a reputation for cruelty and winning at all costs. Despite all of their early morning trainings, Rose wasn’t at all sure Asha stood a chance. Rose had never actually imagined it would come to this and braced herself for disaster.

Rose couldn’t let Asha see any flicker of that doubt in her eyes, and so she focused on the map she was drawing, the ancient map of King Nret.

When all was written Asha looked over the document, her heart bursting with pride at Rose and the perfect words she had used to capture the terms of this very official agreement. Here it was, a description of the borders. Rose had obviously paid attention to her studies. Embedded in the document was a map of Zanzia with the correct boundaries detailed, along with quick lines to show mountain ranges, rivers, and the coast of Zanzia, which Asha had for so long heard of but never seen.

Asha signed her name in large curving letters. Dokar hardly glanced at the document, signing in a flurry, pen pushed deep into the angular letters, heavy with blue ink. Since Rose was officially the scribe, she took command of the signed sheet, deeply afraid that signing this piece of paper would the last thing her dear friend would ever do with her freedom.

7

THE DUEL

"Prepare for the duel!" shouted one of King Dokar's men.

Dokar sized up Asha and licked his lips like a hunter looking at a deer in a trap. In his mind, she was already tied up and slung over the back of his horse, and he was already galloping back to Nadroj. Dokar's men felt the same way. They watched on with a look of amusement and idle boredom. They all knew how this game would end.

They were all slightly annoyed as well. Their horses, swords, jackets, and even their silly hats were now collateral in this wager. This meant that the horses had to be dismounted and corralled, swords (and sheaths too), jackets, and finally hats put into piles. They fussed about the contents of their pockets, already dreading getting their coats mixed up with someone else's. The messy reclamation of their articles was the only complication they foresaw resulting from this sideshow.

Asha gave her crown to Rose for safekeeping. She also removed her outer skirt and the silken flowy piece of her garment. Her remaining skirt had slits up to her waist on either side and was shorter, and underneath her riding pants. She not only looked less frivolous, but her movements were less confined. But she still looked like a girl in a princess dress – and she intended to use that to her full advantage.

Asha feigned difficulty getting her sword out of her leather belt. And when she had it, she held it awkwardly by the guard loop instead of the handle, causing the blade to droop. She practiced a very basic fencing technique, thrusting the blade unevenly with her other hand behind her back. Several Nadrojian soldiers snickered openly behind her, and she knew she must look completely ridiculous. At least she hoped she did.

She knew that swordplay, done properly, was a highly sophisticated art form. Equal parts technique, strength, monotonous practice, and proper mental conditioning. She did not know how much Dokar trained at sword fighting these days. (Everything she knew from Max was six years outdated by now). Dokar certainly looked very strong. Her initial goal was to ensure he was overconfident and not prepared for a competent adversary. (She at least hoped she would be a competent adversary.)

"Let the duel begin!" shouted King Dokar's man.

They touched swords, and Dokar immediately took the first swipe, clearly wanting to make this engagement as short as possible. Asha dodged deftly, and the two began circling each other.

Dokar went for a direct assault. Asha blocked his blade, but not without difficulty. While she was strong, he outweighed her by at least twice as much. The force of his sword required all of her strength. He went in for the same move a second time, appearing to think that her ability to block his sword was accidental. She blocked him a second time, immediately following up the block with a slice to his head, which he ducked, but only barely. He followed this up with a square punch to her stomach with his non-sword hand. This she had not been expecting.

She went flying backward, sprawling on the ground. Her skirt tore, but she did not let her sword out of her hand. All the same, she was sure she had failed and the duel was over. The agreement was that the match would end at first blood. Surely something on her must be bleeding. And even if it wasn't, Dokar would take advantage and be standing over her with his blade tip to her neck. But she was not bleeding, and Dokar had not felt the need to rush over.

So she forged on, leaping to her feet in a single motion, trying to reclaim the rhythm of the sword fight that she knew by heart. She was no longer trying to appear weak and vulnerable. Asha narrowed her eyes in concentration. She noted that the battle had moved slightly, away from the rock. Asha ran directly at the king, sword outstretched. He easily redirected her blow, but in doing so allowed her to reposition herself correctly. It was what she had intended, but what she hadn't expected was what happened when she moved past him.

He punched her square in the face. There was an explosion of pain, and all sound was replaced by a single high-pitched note seeming to come from within her head. She shook her head to clear it, tasting blood (she swallowed it down). She tried to get her bearings, making sure to keep the rock positioned between her and Dokar. Slowly the world came back into focus. Dokar sneered at her, enjoying her evident pain.

He came at her again with a complicated repertoire of movements. Five vicious blows, one after the other. But Asha's heart sang. Max had trained her well during those early mornings in the wet dew. Her feet moved into the correct position automatically. Her blade seemed to rise on its own accord. She parried every blow with perfection. Dokar's eyes grew wide in surprise.

Instinct took over, and Asha returned Dokar's attack with one of her own, unleashing a six-blow attack. Her blade flashed in the light again and again. Dokar defended, but not easily. Her blade sliced the air inches from his face and body. Beads of sweat dripped down his forehead as he cowered under the onslaught.

Asha advanced and struck again.

Dokar tried to parry, tried to sidestep. He kicked out at her, catching Asha in the thigh, causing her to stumble. By now she expected him to fight dirty and absorbed the worst of the blow, rather than be tossed aside by it. But still, it hurt.

"Foolish girl!" he shouted. "You think you are better than me? I'm not even using my sword arm!"

Caught off balance from the kick Asha realized that this was the moment she had been waiting for, and she was going to be too late. She knew what was coming next. Had it just been a few days ago that she had been practicing for this very opening with Max in the palace yard? And yet now she was unprepared. Despite knowing that the kick had ruined her chances, she stayed with her plan (what choice did she have). She ran with all her might to the top of the rock (for this was the entire reason she had been positioning herself to fight next to it) and launched herself off of it.

Dokar had already tossed his sword into the air, exactly as Max had said he might. It twinkled as it spun in the late afternoon sun, as if it was taunting her. Dokar's hand was outstretched, ready to receive it, face set in a sneer of confident victory. If only she had moved a moment earlier! His fingers were already closing in.

Asha leapt upwards off the rock, momentarily distracting the king and breaking his concentration. He looked at her for a moment, but the princess was far away – back in the dawn of four days earlier.

In her head Max's voice rang out. "*Again Asha! Again! Do it again!*"

Her tip found the metal loop of the handle on Dokar's sword. His mouth was agape, not understanding the significance of her strange leap off the rock. Barely clearing the loop guard, she yanked the sword back so the king's blade fell neatly into her other hand. She crossed the blades in front of Dokar's neck. The ping of the two blades crossing was the most beautiful sound she'd ever heard. It meant the fight was over.

She had done it!

For a micro moment, everything went silent. Time seemed to stretch and nearly stop as she took in her surroundings. Dokar's men seemed confused and befuddled. It must have looked like magic, the king's sword materializing in her hand in the blink of an eye.

She took in the image of the king himself, ready to erupt in an explosion of rage.

Even though Asha couldn't see her own army positioned behind her, she could feel their waves of ecstatic joy.

But Asha couldn't celebrate with them. Not yet. The danger for her and her men had just increased precipitously. With one command King Dokar could simply order his troops to slaughter them all. She needed a plan to ensure Dokar honored the agreement.

Asha jumped back up on the rock and curtsied before King Dokar and his army. Speaking loudly, she addressed them all before Dokar had time to give orders.

"Oh, great King Dokar, you have honored us today! I am but an inadequate novice with my sword, but the honorable King Dokar took pity on me! In an act of great generosity, and representing unity between nations, he gifted me his own sword and spared Zanzia the humiliation of losing!" Asha curtsied once more and watched closely for Dokar's reaction.

The king, she knew, was left with two choices: agree that he had thrown her the sword willingly as an act of kindness, or admit he'd been bested by a girl half his size.

Asha quickly interpreted Dokar's silence as acquiescence and pushed on.

"Great King Dokar, we accept your truce offer between our nations! We accept your gifts of swords and horses!" Asha thrusted the king's sword into the air. "And I personally and most humbly accept the gift of your sword! But we would not have you walk home without your coats and hats through the cold mountain pass! As you leave, please take your finery with you! My men will assist you in their return!"

King Dokar had still not moved or spoken, but his men assumed Asha's interpretation of the Kings intentions to be true.

While everyone had seen the act with their own eyes, it had happened so quickly, and in the aftermath – now that the princess was back to being just a princess again, it was easy to think that this was exactly the sort of girl a king would toss a sword to in an elaborate gesture. It was a far more believable narrative than that she had single-handedly defeated the greatest (self-proclaimed) swordsman in their entire kingdom.

The Nadroj army gathered their hats and coats in preparation for the long walk back to Nadroj.

8

ON THE RUN

Rose quickly brought Asha's steed back to her, and the pair rode off grandly toward the main border tent. Asha didn't look back to see Dokar's reaction. There was no time.

She called out names as she went. "Caspian! Dean! Sam! Gregor!"

There were not exactly generals in the Zanzian army, but there were the more senior farmers who kept border operations running smoothly. She called on these men to join her.

Once off their horses and inside the tent, Rose embraced Asha in a hug, her eyes shining. "You did it! That was amazing! You were brilliant!" Rose beamed with joy.

"Prudence, my dear friend," Asha cautioned, her face tight and pale. "My actions today have put us all in extreme danger. The king now knows of my existence. To defeat our entire kingdom, he simply needs to possess one thing – me. He knows exactly where I am, and if there is one thing I know about that man, it is that he is not going to rest until he gets what he wants."

"But what of the agreement?" asked Rose, holding up the parchment with the king's signature. "He said that he will not invade, and he has given us all of our lands back!" She pointed to where Dokar had scribbled his name. "He signed it!"

"The document is valuable. You did a very good job with it, Rose, and we will figure out a good way to use it in time – but not if he gets his hands on me now. Who is going to enforce that agreement?" said Asha with a shaky voice. "Which allies of ours will step in and demand that he follows international treaty law? None have, and none will. We have very little time."

"Just tell us what you need Princess DeBurn," said one of the older farmers named Caspian. His deep voice was filled with a devotion Asha had not heard from him before.

"Thank you, Caspian." She did not have time to reflect on his newfound reverence, though she sure appreciated it. "Dean," she said, turning to a strong man to her right. "I need you to take the large wheelbarrow and fetch hay. Bring the hay into this tent."

Asha turned to another of the men, Sam. "Take two of the war horses down over the hill. Make sure you are well out of sight of here, and that someone up the hill won't be able to see the horses. Make it look like you are deciding which of the two you favor for yourself."

Next she gave instructions to Gregor. "Bring the Thomas twins into this tent. They are the youngest boys here, correct? But don't bring them together. Have them come by one at a time, carrying things.

Lastly, she turned to Rose. "Take the blue silk ream off your dress, go outside. Make sure you are in a spot that has a full wide-open view and make a dramatic show of wrapping your hair in it. Wrap it until none of your hair can be seen, and then come back in."

Her commands were obeyed without hesitation, even though they likely didn't make sense to those carrying out the tasks.

The Thomas twins arrived wearing coarse farming pants and shirts just as Rose returned, her hair wrapped in blue cloth as instructed. The boys were just a little older than Asha, and a bit small for their age.

"Donovan, Vicor," said Asha, "I am going to ask more from you than I possibly have the right. But I am out of time and options, and I think you are possibly the only ones right now who stand a chance of saving our kingdom. But what I need you to do is going to be incredibly dangerous. What say you?"

Donovan spoke first. "Your majesty. We just watched that fight, and I don't care what you said. We saw you beat that

king, Vic and I. We would do anything that you asked."
Victor nodded in agreement.

Donovan and Victor emerged from the tent minutes later wearing the girls' dresses with their heads wrapped in silk. Donovan even had a bit of yellow straw sticking out his headwrap, which Asha hoped would resemble blond hair from a distance).

Thanks to Gregor and Caspian spreading word of Asha's scheme, all the Zanzian men bowed when the costumed Thomas twins came near. Donovan and Victor spent a long time grooming the horse ridden by Asha and Rose, in the open where they could be plainly seen.

Meanwhile, Dean returned with a wheelbarrow of hay. Asha and Rose, now dressed in the pungent clothes of the Thomas twins, jumped in and were covered themselves. Then Dean wheeled them down the slope to where the Nadroj horses were waiting.

The sun began to set over the distant hills. Was it just this morning that they had woken up in their makeshift campsite under the Zanzia sunrise, looking forward to bringing presents to the men? It was already a lifetime away. There would be no rest for them or for the horses that night. They had to put as much distance between themselves and Dokar as quickly as possible. Even in the dark, Asha knew the way.

It was an uncomfortable ride, with no food or extra clothing for warmth. Asha and Rose pushed their horses hard, galloping with haste through woods and the uneven terrain that led from foothills to the rolling meadows. They rode on until they finally reached an inn, which typically meant they had one day's journey left. They slept for a few hours, finally had something to eat, and sent a messenger pigeon back to the castle so the kingdom would be prepared for their return. They left the horses to rest, as their mounts had been pushed hard for two days before reaching the inn and were spent. Less than four hours after they had arrived, Asha and Rose were off again on fresh horses that the innkeeper provided.

The Queen of Zanzia had sprung into action once the messenger bird had arrived. She understood the severity of the changed circumstances better than anyone. They found her waiting for them in front of the castle on a cobblestone terrace. She must have been waiting out in the cool air for hours. Asha, who had been so strong and so resolute this entire time, dissolved into her mother's arms. Rose solemnly handed the queen the agreement with Dokar's deep signature as they went into the dining room to talk.

"I know you are exhausted, my sweet girl," the queen told her daughter, "but if you manage just one visitor, there is someone very anxious to see you."

Max was ushered into the room, eyes alight in joy. Asha ran to him.

"You did so well Asha. I worked you so hard, never thinking you would see this day. You beat him and that makes me so proud and happy." The joy left Max's face, replaced with sorrow. "But it also makes me terrified for you. You have made a great enemy."

"Dokar was always my enemy," Asha replied, defensively. "Nothing has changed."

"Oh, but everything has changed Asha. Dokar is a great man with much pride, and you have humiliated him in so many ways. First, he is humiliated because he knew nothing of you. And then he devised an easy plan to quickly and easily deal with you, and you outsmarted him and outfought him, a double embarrassment. He will hunt you down Asha. I know him. He will never stop until he has ruined you, and maybe all of Zanzia along with you."

"No, don't get me wrong," he said, seeing a look of distress in her expression. "You did exactly the right thing. Better than right. Had you not been there, Zanzia would already be under Nadroji control. Zanzia's era as a kingdom would be over. You saved your kingdom with this act. But in doing so, by defeating him with both your mind and your sword, you have made yourself a marked woman. You can never stop looking over your shoulder. I am so sorry Asha. And I am so proud. Now," he said shaking off the dire warning he had just given. "Before you catch some rest, you have to tell me. I want to hear every moment of your duel with the King Dokar. Don't skip a detail."

. . .

After the girls got a few more hours of sleep, they awoke to find new outfits and identities laid out for them in Asha's bedroom. Asha was provided a messenger's outfit which would be hardy for riding long distances. Rose was dressed also as a messenger but was dressed as a boy.

While the kingdom of Zanzia was now in dire poverty, it had not always been so. Back from a time of grandeur and masked balls came a very strange relic indeed. The queen had found a wig for Asha to help disguise herself. It was a light brown poufy mess that likely was meant to be comical at the time. Asha had seen a baby brown cow once that was overly hairy and very silly looking, and this wig offered the same effect. Asha stuffed her long locks into it, and the frizz rose lumpy and misshapen – as if the cow had slept all night on only one side of its head. Rose, understanding the gravity of the situation and knowing it was a bad time to laugh, did all she could to contain her giggles. Asha tossed her best friend a scowl that only cracked Rose up more.

The queen walked the girls to the courtyard, where the stableboy was waiting with two new horses.

"You know you are no longer safe here," said the queen to Asha. "And you are no longer safe anywhere as yourself. You will leave at once with Rose, back to her homeland, the Kingdom of Pome. You are to say you are siblings. You will stay at the castle, under the protection of Rose's family. But you can never reveal your identity."

The Queen hesitated, seeming to force out the next words. "I know this is the last thing you want to hear, but unfortunately we may have to speed up your wedding day. The prince of the Diamond Isles is to be married in a few weeks in Pome, and they have yet to choose a bride for him. There will be a choosing ceremony to select his wife, which I hope you will attend. I am so sorry, my child, but it is the best way to keep you safe ... and maybe save us all."

Asha eyes flashed with anger.

"That isn't fair! I can protect myself! And I can protect you, too. Dokar doesn't get to decide when I marry. Or whom. I will never grant him that power over me."

The queen sighed. No, it wasn't fair. That they could agree on. But the queen held out hope for a wedding in less than two fortnights.

As Asha said goodbye to her younger sister she asked about this Diamond Island prince. Aurelia was four years younger but spoke with the hushed tones of practiced palace intrigue. Despite her youth, she could always be depended on to have more information about castle secrets than anyone else in Zanzia. She had learned to be invisible in the largely adult world of the castle.

The nine-year-old spoke with a confidence absent in most adults. "Well, usually the ones they are trying to marry off are really old and really fat. Otherwise they wouldn't be so desperate to offer such a powerful dower, like the one that we need. Also, I have heard some wicked things about the Diamond Islanders especially."

"Apparently," Aurelia went on, "the Diamond Islanders were sooo greedy that they mined their island for precious gems to the point nothing was left, and the land just crumbled into the ocean! Also, people say that they are really violent. They say no country will let them stay there because they are so rich and greedy and militant. Since no one feels safe with them around, I heard that no one wants to marry the Diamond Island Prince because they are worried that since the Diamond Islanders already ruined their own country, they are going to just move in to his new wife's country and ruin hers as well, and no one would be able to do anything to stop them because they are such great fighters!"

"Another fantastic catch." Rose whispered to Asha, giving her friend a wink to lighten the mood.

"Oh, don't worry!" Aurelia said upon seeing the stricken look on Asha's face. "You don't have to marry him. You can wait and someone better will come along. You will see!" The sisters embraced. Asha and Rose climbed upon their horses and set off.

"How are you doing?" Asha said to her friend as the castle grew smaller behind them.

"Well," Rose responded, "we are on our fourth set of horses in six days. We keep tiring out the beasts, but we keep going. Also, this outfit is far better than the one I had yesterday.

Less smelly. I keep thinking about poor Donovan in my dress. I hope he found something else to change into!"

Asha smiled. "But does it feel strange to be going home? To Pome?"

Rose looked crossly at Asha. "You know better than anyone Asha, Pome is no longer my home. It will be nice to see my mom again, but I'm a Zanzian girl. I'm going with you so that you can live to fight another day. But there's nothing for me there, except your temporary safety."

9

ANGRY KING

As it turned out, Asha had been right.

King Dokar had indeed sent soldiers back to capture Asha following their duel. His men had done everything correctly, or so they thought. They kept the young princess and her lady-in-waiting in their sights all day long, from a distance. They watched her and Rose tend to the horses, talk to the men, eat dinner around the campfire, and finally settle in for the night. Additional men surrounded the camp, just to ensure that the girls would not be able to escape. Deep into the night they had attempted to kidnap the princess. It was a perfectly-executed plan.

Except that the Nadrojian soldiers burst into the princess's tent only to find two teenage boys fast asleep in cots. The boys awoke confused and said that the princess and her companion were there when they went to sleep. None of the soldiers could remember seeing the boys enter the tent, but then again, they hadn't really been paying close attention to anyone but Asha and Rose. The girls' horses were still there.

"Maybe they went on a walk?" insisted Donovan, rubbing his eyes for effect, doing his best to play dumb, and hide his terror of the guards.

When Donovan and Victor had gone to bed that night, Donovan had taken both of the dresses, wrapped them in burlap and buried them at the bottom of his backpack. The soldiers went through everything but ignored the burlap bundle. King Dokar's men swept the fields for Asha and Rose; certain they would find the two at any moment. But as the night wore on into pre-dawn, it became clear that the girls were gone.

The Nadrojian soldiers were not exactly sure how to bring this news of their failure back to their king. Dokar had been in an especially black mood following 'the event' as they had taken to calling it. They whispered between themselves about the sword fight. Did King Dokar really toss the sword to the princess? That would have been very out of character of their less than generous leader. They did see him throw the sword up in the air, and she had caught it somehow, after launching herself off that rock. Had the pint-sized teenage princess bested Dokar? That seemed preposterous. And why would she not take the credit for the win if she had?

"Well, would you take credit if you had beaten him?" someone asked in a hushed whisper. That answer was obviously a resounding no. Finally, one of the soldiers drew the short straw, and had to tell the king about the missing girls.

The king knew he had long lost the advantage of proximity. He exploded into a rage at the poor soldier who delivered the bad news. The brave soldier stood his ground, responding with the occasional, "Yes, your majesty." But the king's rage was all-consuming, and the soldier who went into King Dokar's tent was never seen or heard from again.

10

ROAD TO POME

It was dark when the girls left the castle, but there would be no sleep for them tonight. They pushed the horses through the woods, each root trying to reach up and grab them. They knew that Dokar's men could catch up with them at any moment, and despite so few hours of sleep over so many days, they pressed on, the adrenaline of fear and escape keeping them awake, while the exhaustion made them always feel on the verge of passing out.

Down through stream banks, up over hills, through rivers. The trail was poor, and the progress was slow, but still they pushed on, eager to put as much distance between them and the clutches of the Nadroj kingdom. The future freedom of Zanzia depended on Asha's liberty in this moment, and they could not be caught.

The girls rode on for three days, hardly ever pausing and jumping in their saddles every time they heard another rider. They stopped at inns for the least amount of time possible, interacting as little as possible with people. On the morning of the fourth day, they awoke before dawn to the pounding of relentless wind-whipped rain. This was the nicest inn they had stayed at. The fireplace in their room made everything nice and cozy, and the outside storm, inhospitable.

"Can't we just sleep in?" Rose grumbled sleepily. "My horse hates me, and he is going to hate me even more in this weather." But even as she said it, she was packing up their belongings. With one more hard push they would make it to Pome today, despite the rain. They readied the horses in the pre-dawn darkness.

The rain never ceased and the road to Pome was muddy and endless. Both horses appeared horrified at what was being asked of them, but they continued on all the same. They were ready to get to the city of Rose's birth. Asha's wig was drenched and itchy, but still she left it on. Both felt safer now, so many days ride away from the reach of Dokar.

Asha heard a sharp whistle from ahead, past a bend blocking her view. The girls quickly took the precaution of taking the horses off the road and into the heavy woods. It was probably nothing, but they were taking no chances.

A moment later a rider passed, hunched over his horse against the weather, in the same direction as they. It was the first person they'd seen all day. Asha heard voices and dismounted, creeping to the edge of the road following the turn. Two riders, the one she had seen, and the one she had heard whistle from around the bend. She inched closer to hear what they were saying.

"Hail Dokar. What news do you have?" said the first man, using a typical Nadrojian army greeting, despite not being dressed in the military uniform. Both men were in heavy oilskin coats.

"I received news by pigeon yesterday with orders to search this road for the princess," replied the second. "I came all the way from Pome today and I've only seen one other person on the road. Some poor fool with a lame horse stuck in the mud, but no sign at all of the princess. It is said she might be traveling with her lady in waiting."

"I have also been searching," said the first man, "and I've come from the other direction. I haven't seen a soul on this road. I suppose there could have been tracks that the rain washed away, but it is hard to imagine that two palace girls could have made it this far by horseback in so little time, and there is no way they would be out in this weather. I suspect they are still back near Zanzia, days behind us." The man paused. "Wait, what was that?"

Both men turned and looked into the woods. Asha was certain they were staring directly at her. She sucked in her breath, not daring to move. She was caught.

One of the men stepped closer to the side of the road, and Asha inched her hand toward her sword, willing herself to stop trembling despite her fear.

After so many days of hard riding and little sleep, and half paralyzed from the bitter rain, she wasn't sure her sword fighting skills would be a match for the brute strength of these large soldiers. These ones looked especially large and strong.

Suddenly a rabbit burst out of the bushes and scrambled across the road. Asha exhaled slowly but kept her hand next to her sword.

"Just a rabbit," said the second man. "You're probably right. No way they'd get this far already. Should we head back towards Zanzia?"

"Yeah," grumbled the first soldier. "There is a decent inn up yonder we can stay at."

The riders headed in the direction of the inn Asha and Rose had only recently departed. Asha forced herself to get up and relay the conversation to Rose. The encounter had been too close, and left Asha shaken. Only the luck of the soldier's whistle had saved them. What had he even been whistling at? She quietly thanked him under her breath.

The girls led their horses back to the road and continued on, hoping no other Nadroj soldiers were further down the road looking for them.

Soon they came across the sight the Nadroji soldier had described: an absolutely miserable man deep in the mud, pulling a reluctant horse that was limping badly. The man made little progress, and it was clear no help would be coming in this weather.

"We have to stop," Asha told Rose.

"The soldiers could be back at any moment," Rose protested in a whisper.

"We have to help him anyway," Asha replied, "For the sake of the horse if nothing else!"

"But what if he is another soldier? What if it's a trap?"

"It's not a trap. I heard the soldiers talking about him earlier. He is not with them; we know that for certain. And I don't think a highway robber would put himself through all of this just to steal a few gold coins."

"We can't be responsible for the welfare of every stranger on the road," insisted Rose.

Asha dismounted and without even saying hello to the man, went to the horse, crouched in the mud, and cradled its injured hoof in her hands. The man did not protest. She took the cap off of a skin of water she carried with her and poured some of it on the injured leg. The reason for the horse's distress was obvious enough. It had somehow managed to get a long splinter in its fetlock, the lower part of it leg. The splinter was long and had pierced deep, so that every time the horse took a step it pushed the sliver of wood further into the leg. the rider hadn't noticed because of the mud, but Asha felt it when she ran her hand over the muddy leg.

She was able to dislodge the splinter without much struggle. The horse was as relieved as its rider was stunned.

"You don't know much about horses, do you?" Asha chided.

"Truthfully, no, if I am to be honest," the young man replied, "But I do know when I'm being saved from my own tomfoolery. I'm not sure exactly what you did, but I am quite certain I owe you a great debt of gratitude." Up close he looked about the same age as them. He was fully soaked and covered in mud.

"Well, we are not quite finished saving you yet!" Asha retorted.

Rose's eye grew. "But your ..." she began, nearly uttering the word *majesty* before catching herself in the nick of time. They had new identities to wear, and those identities had new names, but neither girl was in the habit of using them.

"But Claire," Rose said to Asha, starting over, "I thought we were in a *hurry*."

"You go ahead, brother," responded Asha. "Take this man's saddle. We'll tie his horse to mine, and he'll ride to town on the back of my horse. His mare should be able to walk on that leg, but shouldn't be ridden."

"But is this wise, little sister?" asked Rose, this time choosing her words more carefully. "We know nothing of this man, not even his name. I cannot leave you here."

Asha cringed slightly at the sound of Rose's deep, fake voice, as she tried to sound more like a boy.

"Since I for one am quite in favor of being rescued, let me introduce myself. I am Rowan Overbrook, a bookbinder from Celze. I had this great idea this morning to go for a ride in the rain, and I've spent the last five hours regretting it very much. Especially because, in the words of the lady, I know so little about horses."

Rowan looked hopefully at the girls. A perfect black curl was plastered to his forehead in a comical way, and rain dripped from his nose. The overall effect made him look harmless.

"And I can pay you, too!" Rowan exclaimed. "I can compensate you for your troubles. But not until we get back to Pome, where I am staying."

Rowan smiled earnestly. "I'm freezing, hungry and I'm not too proud to beg on my knees. God knows I certainly can't get any wetter or muddier."

"Brother, take his saddle," Asha told Rose in a tone that would end any further debate. Rose reluctantly moved the items from Rowan's horse to her own.

"I honestly don't know what I would have done if you hadn't come along," he said. "You are only the second person I've seen all day. I didn't think anyone else would be out in this weather."

"I honestly don't know either," said Asha, "which is the only reason we're helping you." She smiled at him in spite of herself. The only threat Rowan posed was to himself, it seemed. And if she couldn't save her kingdom today, at least she could help out this poor, muddy boy.

"All the same, I thank you." Rowan said, taking Asha's hand as she helped him onto her horse.

Asha had ridden with boys on horses before. Resources were scarce in Zanzia and doubling up on horses was common. But it felt different to have this stranger behind her.

As they rode slowly through the storm, Rowan explained from over her shoulder that he was 15 and temporarily living in Pome. He had taken riding that morning to clear his head, underestimating the dreadful weather. He told Asha that the time had come for him to commit to taking over his family bookbinding business, and while he wanted to support his family and he did really love books, he felt there were other things in life he might also be good at.

"Like looking after horses?" Asha teased. Rowan laughed.

They didn't talk much, however, as the rain continued to beat at their faces. Asha thought perhaps she ought to feel unsafe, out here alone with a stranger, as Rose had suggested. But there was something she immediately liked about Rowan, though she couldn't explain why, and his presence made her feel safer somehow.

Rowan was a stranger, but Asha felt an immediate kinship. Like her, he understood well the conflict between doing what your family requires and following your own path in life. In many ways it was why she was on this road, in the mud and rain, on this particular day.

After many more hours, moving slowly to spare the injured mare, they reached the outskirts of Pome. Rowan directed her past several crossroads to the center of town. Asha was in awe of what she saw. She had only known the poverty and quiet decay of Zanzia. Pome was resplendent in contrast. Even on the outskirts, and even in the rain, it felt lively. There was a hustle and bustle as people traveled on horse-back or cart or on foot, all appearing to be having important places to go. The people she saw looked well fed and wore well-made clothing. It was so close to Zanzia, but it felt like such a new and strange place. She wondered if Zanzia had ever been so prosperous.

Rose had promised to send someone to meet her at the main fountain there, but Asha was surprised to find Rose, in a proper dress, red hair unfurled and groomed, standing under an awning with a parasol. It was the most ladylike Asha had seen Rose in ... well, ever.

Asha giggled in delight, and then tried to stop, knowing she couldn't explain any of this to Rowan.

"This is a friend of mine," Asha said of Rose.

"M'lady," nodded Rowan to Rose. Despite meeting her just hours earlier dressed as a boy, Rowan showed no trace of recognition.

This is as far as I can bring you," she told Rowan. "I expect you can make it back to wherever you need to go from here?"

"I can, and I thank you again. You are my guardian angel," said Rowan as he hopped off the horse. Rose, who was trying to keep a straight face at his remark, mouthing 'guardian angel?' behind his back. Asha mouthed back "M'lady," making Rose snicker.

"Hey, girl," Rowan said to his horse, leading her away. "You think you can make it just the short way home again? And then you can rest."

"Can I um... offer you a ride on the back of my steed, your ladyship? Where is your horse?" Asha asked Rose.

"Horse?" scoffed Rose as pompously as she could, twirling her parasol. "I am a lady. I travel by carriage of course. You are to follow us to the castle."

Asha's eyes got big watching her rough and tumble friend walk daintily (extra daintily for effect) to a waiting carriage and climb in. She was already beginning to feel badly for bringing Rose to Pome. She followed Rose's carriage to the castle. She watched in amazement as she approached. Everything about the castle felt so grand and fresh. Well-dressed servants and footmen and guards moved orderly about, and brightly colored banners hung from the outer walls.

11

IN HIDING

As soon they arrived at the castle, and were alone in the stable, Rose exploded. "I was forced to take a hot bath when I got to the castle! Which was lovely, actually, as I was soaked to the bone ... but when I got out my mother had taken all of my clothes and laid out this!" She gestured to her frilly white and pink dress. "And then she sent in someone to do this!" pointing at the enormous bow in her hair.

Asha laughed until her stomach hurt.

Asha's mother had sent a message to Pome that she was to strictly remain in the costume of a messenger servant, but the message had not mentioned Rose, which Rose's mother took to mean her daughter would resume her former role at the castle.

"I almost didn't even recognize you!" was all Asha could say between giggles.

Asha also took a hot bath and put on new, dry clothes, but these were just a much nicer version of the outfit she had worn on her journey. The servants did what they could with the obnoxious wig while Asha was bathing, but it just became a drier version of the fuzzy beige goo it had been when she took it off. With mirrors everywhere, Asha grinned when she saw her ridiculous reflection.

They were dining, alone in the room of Rose's mother, consuming a small feast the matron had brought for them. Asha was delighted to momentarily take her wig off while she waited for her own hair to dry, which always took forever.

"I can't even sit down comfortably!" Rose fumed, perching awkwardly in her fancy dress on the edge of her chair. Asha smiled sympathetically at her friend.

Asha, in keeping with character, slept in a simple but clean room above the stables. Rose stayed with her oldest sister, Grace, so she could more easily tend to her castle duties.

The first night Asha slept deeply, making up for all those missed nights of sleep and the exhaustion of being on the road and on the run for so long. She spent the first day mostly in bed, doing very little, except for replaying the past week and a half and trying to sort out what it all meant.

On the second day she tended to her horse and sent a messenger pigeon to her parents with the agreed upon message, in case it was intercepted. It read:

I have arrived safely in the Padua Mountains, and look forward to being reunited soon.

Rose visited between her "lady's duties," which consisted mostly of endless tea drinking, reading wordy books to well-coiffed children, and managing correspondence letters that all began: "The royal family thanks you for your visit to Castle Pome ..."

The next day Asha woke up early, as she was accustomed to doing, and felt restless. Sword practice in the commons was out of the question. She was in hiding and was not to do anything that would call attention to herself. She was also given strict instructions not to venture outside of the castle walls. After an hour of being awake with nothing to do and nowhere to go, she felt like a caged animal. Hoping it was too early for anyone to miss her, she snuck out through the servant's gate, relieved that no one questioned her. She had never left Zanzia before and was bursting to explore this foreign land.

Out on the streets of Pome, she watched as vendors opened their shops and readied for a new day. After spending so long on a horse and too long in bed, it was delightful to stretch her legs. She wandered aimlessly, until finding a well-worn path through tall grass on the side of the road. She followed it, and when reaching the end her jaw dropped lower than it ever had before.

It was the ocean.

Asha had only heard of it until now. A white strand of sandy beach brushed up against waters more vast than anything she could have imagined. The waves rolled in, gently, in green ebbs and flows. She walked forward, mesmerized at the sheer wonder of it. She breathed in the air, understanding now the strange scent of Pome. It energized her like an elixir. She was drawn to it, and immediately took off her shoes and waded in. The water was colder than she expected, yet soothing. She dug her toes into the sand, holding her skirts out of reach of the waves, enthralled as her feet slowly became buried and as the waves slid into shore one after the other. It was like magic. For a moment nothing at all existed except for her and the sea.

She felt a firm hand on her shoulder.

Asha cursed her own stupidity. Max had warned her not to turn her back. Ever. She let her guard down. She'd left the safety of the castle walls, and soldiers were after her.

Asha unsheathed her sword and spun around to face her accoster, aiming her blade directly at his throat, when a familiar voice called out, "Claire?"

Poor Rowan was frozen in place, Asha's blade grazing the bottom of his chin. He looked completely flummoxed.

"Sorry," he said. "I was calling to you. I guess you didn't hear me?" Before Asha had time to respond Rowan pointed toward the ocean and shouted, "Claire, the wave!" A large roller was headed at them. Asha pulled up her skirt, sword still in hand, and ran up away from the water with Rowan beside her, laughing all the way.

They dropped down on the sand where she'd placed her shoes.

"Thank you for not killing me, although I think you came close," he teased. "And I have learned something important today. I know never to surprise you! Let me start again. Good morning Claire."

Asha had forgotten who she was and shook her head briefly.

You're Claire now, she reminded herself. *Your name is Claire.*

She'd allowed herself to become lost in the ocean and took a second to collect herself and remember her new persona.

"Rowan. You look particularly ... dry today." Rowan was quite handsome, she realized, when not soaking wet and caked in mud. Dark curls framed his rich dark eyes. She quickly looked away so he wouldn't notice she was staring. "How is your poor horse faring?"

"She's much happier back in a dry stable filled with hay compared to riding with me two days ago. I have to confess that I haven't dared to try and ride her again. She gives me the side eye every time I come through."

"I'm sure she doesn't," said Asha with a laugh, as she fumbled and ultimately failed at getting the sand off of her feet so she could put her shoes back on.

"You don't have much experience with beaches, do you?" said Rowan, his eyes twinkling.

"Actually, this is my very first time on a beach," she admitted.

Rowan's eyes grew wide. "Your first time on the coast? Then you have lived a life of depravation!" He stretched his arms as wide as they would go. "Welcome to my version of paradise. Beaches and oceans are truly two of the best things in the world. Purely unaided, you have actually discovered my favorite place in Pome. Here, let me help."

He took out his canteen and rinsed the sand off of Asha's foot. "You know horses, but I know beaches. Now dry it with your stocking and put your boot on before you get more sand on your foot."

Asha did as she was told.

The two walked along the beach for a time, watching the dance as the tide came in. It was much easier to talk here, compared to riding in a monsoon, and Asha asked Rowan if he'd decided what to do regarding the family business.

"That's all I've been thinking about," he confessed. "My uncle just died, so I am expected to take over everything now. If I don't decide now, I'll likely lose the chance to be part of it forever. I mean, it is what I want to do eventually, but I always thought that maybe I'd have a chance to cross a few oceans first."

"Would taking over be that bad?"

Rowan sighed. "With so many orders and so many people wanting to read new books, I'll never get a day off. Book binding all day long, every day for the rest of my life. I wish I could just put it off… for a few years, at least.

He looked out wistfully toward the horizon, as if seeing several adventures waiting out there, beckoning in the morning sunlight, even as he tore his gaze away.

Asha tried to think of some way to agree with him without giving herself away but couldn't. She mumbled, "That must be hard." But she had the same choice in front of her – save her kingdom now, through marriage and altering her life dramatically, or letting her people down.

"All the same, I know I'm quite lucky that there is a family business to take over. I must sound like a whining fool to you. A young man of good fortune that is terrible at counting his own blessings. So enough of my blitherings. More importantly, I have not properly thanked you for saving me. That is, before you tried to kill me. But I take full responsibility for that too. Let me treat you to breakfast."

Asha knew she should get back to the castle. By now it was no longer early, and Rose and likely others would be looking for her. She tried to make herself say no. It was foolish, far beyond foolish she knew, to walk around in the broad daylight while a king thirsty for revenge had sent out hunting parties for her. But also, she knew that there was nothing waiting for her back at the stable except for quietly looking at the four walls. And since she was hungry, and breakfast with Rowan sounded more fun than remaining in hiding, she said yes.

In her disguise, what could possibly go wrong?

12

UNWELCOMED GUEST

Meanwhile, back in Zanzia, Asha's parents were hosting a most unwelcome guest.

The King had made his way to the Zanzian capital of Alba. He did not hurry. He took ten of his men. On the third day the king and queen met him at the gates, and they were prepared. They had trumpeters and banner holders and a freshly butchered cow. They were out of options and were relying on diplomacy and global rules of conduct to protect them. They were frightened, but they hid it from their features.

"King Dokar." The queen said sweetly. "What a delight. To what do we owe this rare visit?"

"Queen Kirsten, King Henrick. I hear congratulations are in order. It appears you have a daughter."

"Oh yes!" said the Queen. "Asha mentioned that she had met you. She spoke of your kindness and generosity. Has it been that long since we have seen you last? We thought you must have heard the news ages ago, but your kingdom is indeed far away. We should have sent a messenger."

"Asha," Dokar said, darkly. "Where is she? I was quite taken with her and would love to see her again." He looked around the courtyard, as if she might join them at any moment, though deep down he knew the girl was gone.

"Oh no," said Queen Kirsten, a bit too brightly. "She has gone away for the remainder of the school year. We want to make sure she receives an education befitting royalty. But I'm sure we can arrange a visit when she comes back. We will send someone to let you know as soon as she returns."

"I'm sure you will." Dokar spoke slowly, with silences between words at times, tinging the very words themselves with danger. "You must be very proud of such a daughter. Tell me, have you selected a proper suiter? Have you considered what it could mean for Zanzia if you betrothed her to someone in Nadroj? Perhaps ... someone ... like me."

"Oh we are so very honored your majesty! That is a very generous offer indeed." The queen gave a curtsy in an attempt to convey the sincerity she did not feel, as she shuddered inwardly. "Of course as you know she is still such a young girl. She is only 13. You know how kids are these days, no longer willing to be married off so young. When the time of her matrimony comes closer, in four or five years from now, will gladly revisit this offer."

"It would be a wonderful way to unite our two kingdoms," said Dokar, never breaking eye contact.

That evening they held a feast, although no one had cause to celebrate. Food was scarce in Zanzia, and it seemed like such a waste to use for this awkward, precarious occasion. But that was part of the point as well. To make it appear to Dokar that they were not so wanting and desperate and poor. And that he did not have as much power over them all as he clearly did. King Dokar picked at his poorly-seasoned steak silently, appearing ready to explode at any moment.

13

THE BOOKCASE CAFE

The place Rowan took Asha for breakfast was more library than restaurant. Every wall was lined with books, with tables set up on various landings. Books were scarce in Zanzia, making them almost as precious as gold and jewels. Asha stood breathless and soaked it all in. So much richness, so much knowledge, and all in one place!

Rowan noticed her wonder. "Isn't it fantastic?" It's another of my favorite places. You are getting the full tour of my favorite places today it seems. You can eat and read to your heart's content. And there is often lively discussion as well," he added, nodding in the direction of two men of about Rowan's age speaking passionately and pointing at something one of them was reading.

Rowan spoke to the waiter and soon their table was overflowing with thick slices of fresh-baked bread, lingonberry jam, a wedge of smoked salmon, crisp slices of thickly-cut bacon, clotted cream, lemon curd, eggs sunny side up, a pot of coffee, and fresh orange juice. It was all Asha could do not to inhale the entire table's worth of food. She had grown up in a castle that served pauper's meals. This was the richest spread she had ever experienced. She tried to treat her meal with the indifference that everyone else in the café seemed to have, but her mouth would not stop watering and it was all she could do not to stuff enormous bites into her mouth. But when she remembered she was in disguise and wouldn't be judged on her table manners (for once) she gave up holding herself back and dug in with joyful abandon.

She followed Rowan from the table, and they each grabbed several books off the shelves, and they spent the morning eating, reading and talking. Soon the nearby discussion rose in volume.

"People should marry for love and only for love!" argued the man sitting nearest to Asha. "These arranged marriages go against everything natural to mankind. Business arrangements can be just that, business arrangements. But marriage is about passion and companionship."

Rowan smiled at Asha as they both listened.

"Nonsense, Marcus!" said a second man in a green hat. "Marriage is nothing but a necessary agreement to transfer power and wealth. When power and wealth are of short supply, then by all means marry for love. But you cannot expect royalty to marry whomever they choose. What would happen to world order? These are the decisions that shape and maintain the structures of our society and countries, as they should be. Without properly selected matches, kingdoms would descend into chaos."

"You are cold hearted!" Marcus protested. "Love isn't practical and transactional. Humans were created to live for love. We attract and are attracted to others based on the mysterious and wonderous laws of the universe. How can you say that the contracts of man are better suited to determining coupling? All society would be better off if there was more self-determination." He pointed to Asha. "You there ... don't you think love and romance is more important than wealth and power when choosing a husband?"

Asha hesitated at first to speak but realized that while in disguise she could finally speak freely on this very subject that had so long occupied her thoughts.

"You are both correct....And incorrect," she said decisively.

Marcus laughed. "Now that is not an answer at all. We have entirely different views. You cannot agree and also disagree with both of us. Please explain."

"Gladly," said Asha. "When a princess is forced to marry, and not for love, do you feel sorry for her?"

"Of course!" Marcus vehemently agreed. "And for the poor chap she doesn't want to marry as well!" he added with a chuckle.

"So," said Asha, "moving that argument forward. Do you also feel sorry for a soldier who goes out and fights for his country? Or let's take it up a level, what about the general who leads his soldiers to battle. Do you feel sorry for him, leading his troops?"

"No, of course not, but that's different. I don't see your point. You are talking about war, while we are talking about matrimony." Marcus grinned, welcoming further debate.

"Ah, but they are very much the same," Asha insisted. "A soldier is willing to give his life on the battlefield. But his singular death will have only a small impact, correct? The general, on the other hand, can do more. He commands a larger group of troops, but the end goal is the same. Soldiers and generals do their part to keep their people safe and to ensure the prosperity of their kingdoms. But a princess who is being given away in an arranged marriage, her impact is greater still. With the simple act of marriage, she can have the same impact as tens of thousands of soldiers and hundreds of generals, all willing to give their lives. A royal marriage can result in lasting peace without the need for bloodshed."

All three men stared at her for a moment and pondered.

"So," said the man in the green hat, a grin spreading across his face, "what you're really saying is that I win the argument!" He stood up from his chair and bowed to their small group. "She agrees with me!"

"Well, no. At least not entirely." Asha, replied. "Marriage should be for love whenever possible."

The man in the green hat sat down dramatically, clutching his hand over his heart as if he had been shot, much to the amusement of the small assemblage

Marcus gestured an elated see-I-told-you-so expression to those watching.

"Arranged marriage should only occur if it is in replacement of war, or dramatically helps a kingdom's strategic advantages," Asha continued. "If these people are to give their lives for a greater public good, the sacrifice of their personal lives needs to mean something. And most importantly, arranged marriages should never involve children. No one sends children to war. It should be the same for nobility."

"I like this girl!" said Marcus.

"Me too!" said his friend. "It's so nice to finally talk with someone with some sense who agrees with me for a change."

The two men went back to arguing again – but this time over who Asha had agreed with more strongly.

Rowan whistled quietly under his breath. "Impressive. I've never thought of a royal marriage in that way. You're an interesting girl, Claire. You're as sharp with your intellect as you are with a sword, it seems."

Asha glanced around the room, avoiding Rowan's eyes – he mustn't see her blush – and spotted an abandoned chess board on a nearby table.

"Do you play chess?"

"Actually, I love chess!" he said.

As Rowan fetched the board and set up the pieces, she grabbed the last slice of bacon. Bacon was definitely her new favorite food.

Rowan was a surprisingly good chess player. He somehow managed to capture her queen, but she snuck a pawn through his defenses to get it back, abruptly check mating him. Instead of looking wounded he grinned happily. "It seems I have met my match! You are full surprises Claire."

Too many hours had slipped by. She forced herself to say goodbye to Rowan, almost certain she'd never see him again. Leaving the castle had been too risky, and she dared not venture outside the castle walls again.

Rowan didn't make it easy for her, however.

"When will I see you next?" He smiled at her, and Asha found it difficult to say never.

"I don't know. Are you going to need recusing again anytime soon?" she said, smiling back.

"There is a waterfall in the nearby hills I've been wanting to checkout. Mostly I want to see if my horse will ever allow me to ride her again. So I may indeed need a chaperon. Join me day after tomorrow?"

Against her better judgement she agreed.

Asha found Rose waiting at the stables, her face as red as her hair.

"Where were you!?" scolded Rose. "I checked in and you were gone! You do realize you're a wanted fugitive with the whole Nadroji army out looking for you. I was so worried!"

Not even a stern Rose could deter the merriment in Asha's face.

Rose relented. "Fine, tell me everything."

And Asha did, mostly, paying great detail to the ocean and the many wonderful foods she'd eaten for breakfast, while deemphasizing her interactions with Rowan. And she said nothing of their plans for a future encounter.

Asha was enjoying her time in Pome, but that enjoyment brought guilt. Casting aside her role as royalty meant she could be anyone, say anything. For the first time she began to understand what it meant to be free.

There had been no news from Zanzia, and for all she knew her country was in an all-out war. Yet here she was, playing on the beach, feasting, and making plans to go sightseeing.

That evening she sent another pigeon to her parents. The message read: *The Padua Mountains are lovely this time of year, but I am eager for news.*

Of course, she was nowhere near the Padua Mountains, but her family would know this meant she was safe.

14

GAMES

King Dokar and his contingent did not appear to be winding down their time as guests at the Zanzian capital anytime soon. Queen Kirsten forced herself to carry on a cheerful demeanor, playing the role of the perfect hostess as the days wore on. She reasoned that no good could come from calling a spade a spade in this particularly delicate situation.

As long as everyone treated King Dokar as a welcomed guest, and not as an invader, then perhaps nothing terrible would occur.

"Peace through niceties," she said to herself like a mantra, pasting back on the grin that was hurting her face.

"At least he did not bring Commander Blackwell with him." King Henrick told his wife. "I hear he is back keeping order in Nadroj. He is more ruthless than Dokar and might have slaughtered us all already."

"Well, at least there is that. We haven't all been slaughtered yet." Queen Kirsten responded to her husband, cheerily.

Queen Kirsten apologized profusely to her guests when the butchered cow had been fully consumed, and they went back to their more standard Zanzian fare of mashed gruel and boiled potatoes absent any seasoning. King Dokar was not used to going without fine fare and immediately sent a couple of his men to trade in the nearby Kingdom of Trask to bring back some proper food. This turned out to be more complicated than he originally thought.

Since he had made trade into Zanzia punishable by death, the Traskians were not eager to test the Nadroji King's leniency in this one case. When his men retuned empty handed, King Dokar, much to his own annoyance, signed a new piece of parchment nullifying the ban on trade with Zanzia. Only then did he get his food order.

The second time, King Dokar's men returned with pheasants, cranberries, acorn squash, fresh sea bass and blocks of butter and hunks of chocolate. They came with salt, pepper, rosemary, and paprika –all of it handed over to the palace cooks. King Henrick and Queen Kirsten dined with King Dokar that evening, amused for the first time in so many weeks. There were so many things to worry about, but at least the trade embargo had been lifted for the moment and the stuffed chocolate cranberry pheasant was the best meal that had been served in the castle in nearly 20 years.

With a full belly, Queen Kirsten observed King Dokar. He was a truly terrible man, to be sure – obviously a result of neglect as a child. She felt no sympathy for him, or forgiveness, but that night she invited him to join in their evening card game of Euchre. She reasoned that he was a man who had very little play in his life, and very little practice working with others.

Queen Kirsten arranged so that Dokar would be her partner, and for her and Dokar to win the game.

He snorted with glee when they won. It was not a graceful victory. But he was happy, and keeping Dokar happy was the point.

Keep him distracted, Queen Kirsten told herself. *Keep him occupied and somehow this might all work out.*

The Queen's thoughts turned to her daughter and the hope that maybe Asha would relent and marry the Diamond Island Prince, and... but she pushed that thought aside. Even the Diamond Islanders couldn't save them now. King Dokar was here and he could choose to take Zanzia at any moment.

She felt like they were but a few hands of Euchre away from losing the entire kingdom.

15

PIGEONS

Princess Aurelia remained hidden and out of sight. She dressed in black and clung to the shadows and small spaces, putting her long learned spying skills to work. Her hair was worn in the two brown braids. She was the one who saw Dokar and his men sneak into the pigeon roost just as a bird was landing. And she was the one who saw him take the message ("it must be from Asha!" she thought).

Dokar wrote his own note and attached it to another pigeon and tossed it out into the sky. Aurelia tried to think of what message the king would have sent. Perhaps he wrote an official message from Zanzia to trick Asha into coming home, she wondered. Or perhaps he threatened to hold Zanzia hostage unless she returned.

She could picture the message in her head: *We have your family. Come home at once!"*

And Asha would come. Aurelia was sure of it. Regardless, any message sent by Dokar would not be good for Zanzia or for Asha.

The pigeon was one Aurelia had trained herself, with grain from her own hand. It was one of her favorites. But when it soared into the sky, there was only one thing to be done.

She notched an arrow, and when Dokar and his men turned away she released it. Her arrow flew true, a little too true, and hit its target perfectly. A tear leaked out of Aurelia's eye.

She'd taken the pigeon's life to keep it from reaching her Asha. "I'm so sorry Hugo bird," she mumbled under her breath.

Her only consolation was that she had been correct in doing so.

The message attached to Hugo's leg read:

Asha,

I have your family and am holding them hostage. If you come home, I will release them in exchange for you. But hurry, as I may decide to kill them if you do not make haste.

– King Dokar

Aurelia was glad that Asha had not received the message. What she wasn't sure of was whether Dokar was making empty threats or real ones. Obviously, she and her family were in danger, but was he really planning to kill them? She had to do something, but what? What could any nine-year old do?

She was good with her bow, but she vowed to never use it in that way ever again. The one thing Aurelia understood was that controlling the flow of information was a powerful thing. Aurelia had learned this in the palace. She was also good with the pigeons. It was she who had given them names and helped train them. Alec, the castle's animal minder, called her a natural.

No matter how long King Dokar stayed, Aurelia knew he would need to use the messenger pigeons.

The best thing she could do was to retrain the pigeons. They were trained to come to the coop and leave from it for specific places. She'd train them to make one extra stop along the way from the coop. It would only work if they didn't have to go very far. She could do this. But she had to act fast and remain invisible.

First, she needed to get a message to her sister.

Dear Asha,

We are safe and hope you are well. Dokar's men are looking for you. Be careful! Stay well-hidden. That's an order!

– Aurelia

She attached the note to the leg of a pigeon she'd named Esmerelda, opened the coop and let Esmerelda fly free.

"Good luck Esme," she whispered into the sky as the bird disappeared from view. Aurelia knew she'd managed to buy her sister more time, but how much she did not know.

After that Aurelia had a very sad, very lonely funeral for Hugo the messenger pigeon. She recited a poem about a fallen soldier by his grave and promised him his service to Zanzia would not be forgotten.

16

WATERFALL

Asha met Rowan two days later at the beach she previously discovered. Sneaking out of the castle grounds on horseback proved quite a bit harder than on foot. She arrived late to find Rowan cantering through the waves. She watched from a distance, as he splashed with his horse in the water before galloping at full speed to join him in the spray. Together they charged back and forth, laughing, along the incoming tide.

It was a lovely day. The sun warm but not hot, they made the long trek into the hills on the southeastern side of Pome.

They talked, but it was becoming increasingly difficult for Asha to tell stories, since she couldn't reveal anything true about herself. And then there was keeping track of all the falsities. It was easier to talk about other people.

She told Rowan about Rose, but called her an older sister named Daisy (since he had already met the real Rose earlier) and talked about Aurelia as a younger, spunky sister named Freyja.

Despite her royal roots, her poverty was real enough. It hadn't been too hard to concoct a story of how she had been a royal messenger in Zanzia, mostly delivering messages between the capital and the northern border contingent. That part was true. And so, she told him of the wide-open sky and the vast, empty hills and fields. She told tales of camping under the stars, and the Northern Lights.

Rowan mostly spoke of his love of the ocean. His family's printing business was near the sea, and he grew up loving the aroma of ink and the salty smell of waves on an ocean breeze. He loved to fish and could spend hours with his rod catching dinner for the evening.

"Once I tried to print an entire book with octopus ink," he told her. "The ink bled terribly and that oozing black stuff took forever to clean up." Asha laughed at his description of the mess.

They tied up the horses when finally arriving at the waterfall. They took off their shoes to get as close as possible and saw the outlines of a cave behind the waterfall. They dared each other to get closer, before both dashing in, now able to look at the world they had just departed through sheets of liquid torrents. By the time they were able to pull themselves away, the sun was much lower in the sky than they had intended.

As they walked back to their horses, Asha felt a pang of trepidation for leaving the tall castle walls. A lump formed in the back of her throat and her stomach felt like a sequence of knots.

Something was amiss.

Just then two men stepped out from the trail in front of them, swords drawn. Instinctively Asha put her hand on Rowan's arm, pushing him back.

"Rowan get behind me!" she hissed. "I'll protect you."

Rowan was nearly a foot taller than Asha and outweighed her significantly. He looked at her incredulously, shaking his head. "Claire, this is not the time. *You* get behind *me*."

They locked eyes for a moment and a firm understanding passed between them. The understanding of fellow warriors. The resolve in Rowan's face and posture told Asha he could handle himself just fine. A movement attracted her attention.

"Rowan! Two more!" she shouted as men came at them from behind.

Rowan and Asha went back to back as if they had practiced it a thousand times.

Rowan drew the long wooden rod he always carried on his back. Asha had noticed it, of course, and had commented on it, but he had laughed it off, saying bookmakers carry sticks instead of swords, so that they don't accidently poke themselves. She had thought it was hilarious at the time, but now he drew that wooden rod like he was an assassin, and she understood that this was his weapon of choice. She didn't have time to observe, however, with two sword fighters coming directly at her.

She noticed these four men didn't belong to Dokar, which offered a small amount of relief. They held their swords like they were planning on cutting brush, relying on the intimidation of their approach rather than any real technique. She could hold both of them off easily on her own but gasped when she saw another assailant emerge from behind a bush, making it five in all.

"Are you okay, Claire?" Rowan was busy holding off three men with swords with his spinning deadly rod.

"I'm good. I just wish I had an extra sword right about now!"

"Give me a second!" Rowan grunted. Asha heard a thump and a yelp. "Claire, sword! Top left." Like magic a sword materialized from above her left shoulder, dropping effortlessly into her waiting hand.

Now that she had two swords, she battled both of the armed men simultaneously. She parried and engaged. The men grunted and dodged, clearly exhausting themselves, while Asha hit her stride.

The swordplay felt comfortably familiar. It reminded her of training sessions with Max, when he'd make her practice with the farm boys.

Both men were trying their hardest, but she held them off effortlessly. A third man approached. She needed to do something quickly. Dueling against three swords was not her strongest skill, as she didn't have the necessary height or reach.

Asha reviewed her options and grinned widely. The first two men looked nervously at her, despite seeming to have every advantage.

Back in Zanzia, Max had taught her a move that she had never had a chance to try in an actual fight because she never wanted to hurt the good-natured farm boys that sparred with her.

She let the memory of Max's words flow through her.

'You have to draw them each into a sword play that must be choreographed and symmetrical. You become their puppet master. Have them stand as close together as you can make them, while engaging each just above your shoulder – one on the right, and one on the left. Pick your moment. You are a conductor, conduct them! Slash in with each of your swords at once. Now Asha, you are not trying to decapitate them. You are a warrior, not a killer. They will think you are fast, but of course you are not using your full speed. Both will draw back their heads at the same time, away from the swords, and...'

BONK!

The two men who had ambushed her slammed their heads into one another hard enough to knock themselves out cold. They lay on the ground before her in crumpled heaps. She took a moment to appreciate her own handiwork, before turning her full attention to the new assailant.

The smiling third man found himself unexpectedly facing her all by himself, his grin instantly dissolving. He wore a wide hood, giving Asha an idea. He began backing up. Asha gave him a few steps before she took aim, transferring the "borrowed" sword into her right arm and using it like a javelin. She let it fly. The hooded man yelped, and she hoped for his sake he would not move too much. The sword grazed his cheek, embedding itself in his hood, and pinning him into the tree directly behind him. As his head swung back, hitting the tree, he knocked himself out cold as well.

Asha heard a booming, delighted laugh and turned to find Rowan standing over two disarmed and unconscious swordsmen, stick still in one hand, other hand on his belly laughing in wonder and surprise at the three men she had singlehandedly dispatched.

Asha didn't share his amusement. "Rowan, we have to get out of these woods!"

But Rowan was still chuckling as they stepped over limp bodies on the ground to retrieve their horses. "Claire, you took out three armed attackers without getting even a scratch!" said Rowan, studying her and shaking his head incredulously.

"They were only common roadside thieves" she replied, as if this explained everything.

"Also, nice stick Rowan," she said, raising an eyebrow significantly. "You have made me reassess my choices in life. I've decided not to try to take on any bookmakers in a fight. Who knew you typesetters could be so vicious!" He laughed again and she nudged him in the ribs.

Silently though she was still berating herself for being so reckless. By now Dokar had likely put a bounty on her head. One that described her as a sword fighting lass, and she had just clearly demonstrated to five ne'er-do-wells exactly who they should be on the lookout for and had given them lots of clues of where to find her. Her poufy wig disguise was now probably useless. She cursed herself and bit her bottom lip. She might as well be announcing to the entire world she was in Pome.

They made their way in silence on horseback for a time before Rowan finally spoke.

"Claire, I've been wanting to talk to you about something." Uncertainty in his voice. "I don't know if now is a good time for it. I don't know what you are going to say, but I've been thinking about it a lot. There is a ship leaving next week for Dumas," he said, his words rushing together.

"Do-where? Do what?"

"Dumas. It's a land that my ancestors are from. I've never been there, and I've always been curious about it."

"Wait," said Asha. "I thought you told me that you were about to take over the family business."

Rowan kept his eyes down on the ground in front of him. "Yes, I told you that. So, this would be instead of that. Before that."

"Are you running away?" Asha pressed on. "Does your family know?"

"They know I'm unhappy. They know the business is more than I really want to take on right now."

"Are you going to tell them? Before you go?"

"I was considering not telling them. But now that I say it out loud, and seeing you look at me like that, it sounds worse than when I just thought it in my head."

"I'm not looking at you like anything," Asha asserted. "I'm just trying to understand what you are saying."

"I had planned to leave a note, which again doesn't sound very good aloud. I'm supposed to take over the family business. And it's a good company, and a great family, but I just don't think it's what I want to do right now. It's always been the plan and I never had a choice one way or another, so I'm just finally exercising my right to choose what I want for once."

"You don't have other brothers or sisters who could take over? Or cousins?"

"Second cousins are the closest, and they didn't grow up in the business, so they don't know it at all. It has to be me. But I want...more. I just don't know how to tell my family. I thought that maybe all I needed was a bit of an adventure.

So, I go to Dumas, do some sightseeing, and then maybe I'll be ready. It's not like they can't run the company without me. They have been doing just fine all these years. I'll come back when I'm ready and take over then."

Asha wanted to tell him to talk to his family. Maybe they'd see his side. But that hadn't worked for her, so who was she to give advice.

Running away, in truth, sounded very tempting.

They rode in silence for some time, until Rowan said, "You could come with me."

"What?" said Asha, taken aback.

"Yes. I've been thinking about it," Rowan said quickly. "I know we've just met, but I feel like you are like me, in need of an adventure. You're a messenger, so you could go. You would not be abandoning anyone, right? You never even had a chance to see the ocean before. I thought maybe you would want a chance to see more of it."

"*Me*?! You want me to come *with* you?" Asha was still caught up in the initial comment.

"Well, yes," Rowan said, who this whole time had been staring down the path. "I mean, I know it's crazy. But I was hoping. I mean, if you want to," he stammered.

Asha didn't trust herself to speak. And so, the silence hung between them as they rode until Rowan finally broke it. "The boat doesn't leave until Friday. You can take some time to think about it." Finally, he turned to her. "But Claire, I do hope you will come." Asha imagined being on a boat, sailing far away from the madness which was her life. Not alone, but with her new friend, and in a place where no one was hunting her. It was a tempting offer.

An approaching group of riders shocked her back into the present moment. It was Nadrojian soldiers, she was sure of it. Four of them, traveling as a unit, coming from the direction of Pome. Adrenaline filled her.

"Rowan" she whispered. "I need you to do something for me. If they ask you questions, tell them I'm your sister, and that you don't let me speak to men."

Rowan, confused by this abrupt transition, seemed to absorb what she said only as the contingent began to pass.

"Greetings!" one of the soldiers called out. "May I have a word?"

"Certainly," replied Rowan, amiably. "How can I be of service?"

"We are searching for two young ladies who are of interest to our king. Perhaps you have seen them. Princess Asha has long blond hair, and her lady in waiting Rose has long red hair." The soldier's eyes fixed in Asha. "Perhaps *you* have seen them m'lady."

Asha froze when the soldier spoke her name, her true name. She gazed back at him with blank, expressionless eyes.

"I don't let my sister, Buttercup, speak to any man but me," apologized Rowan. "I'm sure she hasn't seen anyone that fits that description, because I certainly haven't, and she is not allowed to be unaccompanied. Buttercup? Have you seen a blond princess or a red-headed lady?"

"No, my brother," Asha murmured, looking down.

"There you have it," said Rowan. "We will be sure to keep our eyes out. Why did you say you were looking for them?"

"I didn't," the soldier responded curtly, urging his horse on to catch up with the other soldiers who had continued on.

Once they were a safe distance away, Asha glared at him.

"Buttercup?!" she said incredulously.

Rowan laughed. "Well, you had mentioned your sister Daisy earlier, and then he said that he was looking for someone named Rose, and so I could only think of flower names. It was the only name I could think of. I could hardly keep a straight face! Wait, but why did you want me to tell them you were my sister?"

"Oh, it's silly. I was given strict orders not to take the horse outside the castle walls today, and I thought they were Pome soldiers and I might be in trouble," Asha made up quickly.

"Weren't they Pome soldiers?" Rowan asked.

"They wore the Nadrojian insignia," she explained. "I've delivered messages there in the past and recognized it."

"Nadroj," Rowan mused. "They certainly are far from home. I wonder what they are doing so far away in these parts. What about this princess Asha. Ever heard of her?"

Asha considered saying she hadn't, before remembering she was pretending to be a royal messenger from Zanzia, and it would appear strange if she didn't know the Zanzian princess.

"Asha is the next in line to the Zanzian throne," she confessed, choosing her words carefully. "But when I left Zanzia she was still there." She felt oddly proud that everything she said was technically true, yet utterly false at the same time.

"But I thought Zanzia only had princes. I read a book about Zanzia once," he said.

"It wasn't a very accurate book then. I hope you were not responsible for printing it. There is not a single Zanzian prince. Only princesses."

"Maybe it's time to commission a new book on Zanzia." After a moment he said, "So, are you thinking about coming with me to Dumas?"

"I am. Thinking about it," Asha replied.

"You are?" Rowan grinned broadly.

"*Thinking* about it," she emphasized.

They were at the servants' entrance now, and she knew she should go in.

"Rowan, I think I'm going to be in trouble for leaving the castle by horse when I wasn't supposed to," she told him, knowing that with all the Nadroji soldiers prowling around Pome, it would be beyond foolish to wander freely again. "I don't know when I will be able to see you again. But look here …" she pointed to a loose rock on the outer wall. "This crack goes all the way through, and if you leave a note for me here, I will write you back."

"Well then, I will write you," Rowan pledged.

Asha smiled. And they stayed like that, smiling at each other, until the guard asked if she was going in. Asha regretfully tore herself away and disappeared under the stone arch.

17

LETTERS IN THE WALL

Asha returned to find Rose sitting on her narrow bed above the horse stables. "Where have you been? I've been worried sick about you! You know you were not supposed to leave the castle grounds. Anything could have happened to you..." She stopped mid-diatribe as she caught the expression on Asha's face. "Okay, fine. There is something going on with you. Out with it!"

And Asha did. She told her about sneaking out to meet Rowan, the waterfall, and the attack by the highwaymen (although she downplayed it immensely). She glossed over the encounter with Dokar's men. Finally, she told Rose that Rowan had invited her to join him on a ship to Dumas and he was leaving on Friday.

"He wants you to go with him!?" Rose exclaimed. "He invited you to run away with him, and you didn't say no? Are you crazy? Is he crazy?"

"I don't know Rose... maybe. All I know is that I wanted to say yes." Asha smiled at her friend hopefully.

"Oh, dear Asha. Listen to you. You like this boy, and a little too much, I think." There was concern in Rose's voice.

"No, I don't!" Asha protested. "But Rose ... he's so fun to talk to and just...different from anyone else I've known before. I wear this wig when I am with him and half the time I forget to turn around when he says 'Claire.' I must seem like an idiot for not even knowing my own name. But I've never felt so much like myself before. Do you think I should go?"

"On a boat? With him? To someplace called Dumas we've never heard of? No, of course I don't think you should go! Even to consider it is mad," Rose scoffed. "You are the last chance to save Zanzia. You know that."

"Yes, but maybe that is precisely why I should go!" Asha argued. "Think about it. No one will suspect that I've gone seafaring. King Dokar can't kidnap me and use me to steal Zanzia. No one will look for me in Dumas. I'll be safe there." Asha hoped she sounded convincing.

"Safe but for what purpose? You are to marry a king, Asha, and the sooner the better. What happens to all of Zanzia if you're off on an island somewhere with your new boyfriend."

"He's not my boyfriend, and I'm pretty sure that Dumas is not an island," Asha protested, realizing that she had no idea, which didn't improve her argument.

"It doesn't matter, Asha! That's not the point. The point is that there is a kingdom's worth of people depending on you to save them. And now you are talking of running away?" Rose added a bit more softly. "You know you can't, right?"

"Oh Rose, don't be silly. I didn't tell him yes, it was just a fun thing to think about, that's all," Asha said, brushing the whole conversation aside.

"He's just a boy. A handsome and likable boy, but still just a boy. Keep your eye on the bigger prize. All of Zanzia is depending on you."

"I know," Asha said. "I am."

But that night she dreamed of sailing across the ocean with Rowan. He was next to her on the deck of a ship, the open ocean and sky spread out before them. She smiled in her sleep all night long.

The next morning she woke early, as the dawn's streaks were just brightening the horizon. She snuck out to check the crack in the wall near the castle's entrance. She expected to find it empty, but when she removed the loose rock the edge of a piece of paper greeted her. She took the note and raced back to her room to read it.

Dear Claire,

I hope you have not had to beat up any roadside thieves since last we met. That was quite a show you put on! Someday you will have to tell how it is you are such an impressive sword fighter.

Tomorrow I will be booking myself a room on the M/V Intrepid. I can book you one as well, if you decide you want to join me across the ocean.

Yours fondly, Rowan

The letter certainly had not quelled the mixed up and confused emotions dancing inside her. And her confinement within the castle gave her nowhere to go, and no way to distract herself from thinking about Rowan's letter.

Should she go?

After reading the letter again, Asha finally took a parchment of her own and began a letter to Rowan. She crumbled up several pieces of paper before she settled on the following:

Dear Rowan,

The obvious answer is no, of course.

But I cannot bring myself to say no just yet. I will not answer your question at all, because it is even more impossible that I tell you yes.

And so, I will ask you nothing about Dumas or what it is like to cross an ocean. Instead tell me this – how did a bookmaker learn to master the – stick? Rod? What is it that your weapon is called, and how did you become so good at it? Also, why would you ask a girl you had just met to sail across the ocean with you? It is a ridiculous question. But one I still do not have a response to.

Claire

Dear Claire,

I am glad you are at least considering thinking about coming with me. I will help you with your quandary. You don't have to say yes or no at all. Just meet me Friday morning before dawn at our beach before sunrise. I'll be waiting.

As for why I am good with a weapon, I'm afraid I was completely outdone by your prowess with a sword, so I can hardly take your compliment seriously. Maybe I should just "stick" with my books.

Speaking of books, I am packing several for you for our journey. Some on philosophy, a couple histories, and a very good novel. I think you will like them as much as I do.

I can't wait to see you,

Rowan

Dear Rowan, -

How many books did you pack for me? I'm starting to suspect this might be a very long journey. Maybe it is time for me to ask more questions. How far away is Dumas exactly? Also, I didn't actually defeat anyone with a sword. The three poor thieves just bonked their heads and knocked themselves out cold. I mostly just watched the spectacle.

Tell me more about Dumas.

Thinking about it,

Claire

But no matter how many times she checked the chink after that, there was no response, and none of the following letters that she hid in the wall were taken. They sat there, and she stared at them, unable to extract the meaning of their continued presence, and the continued absence of any further word from Rowan. Had something happened to him? Had the Nadroji soldiers found out he had been with her and captured him? Her heart pounded to think that something bad had happened to him. But the empty stones held no answers for her.

18

SUBTERFUGE

Aurelia was having excellent luck retraining the pigeons. It helped that all they had to do was fly to a nearby tree, get a treat, and pause for a moment before continuing their journey. Remaining invisible to King Dokar and his soldiers while trying to retrain the birds proved trickier. Dokar's men occasionally checked the roost for new messages. Also, the pigeons would only come to the tree if Aurelia was in it. This meant Aurelia was now spending most of her time hanging out in a tree.

The first message came after a tedious six hours in the tree. Her left arm had fallen asleep, and she'd taken to counting leaves to keep herself alert, when she heard Dokar's men approach the coop. Soon after a pigeon alighted on her arm in a flurry of feathers. She took the message attached to the bird's foot and read it. The message was a command from King Dokar.

Good intel that Asha has been spotted in Pome. Remain there, secure the girl, and bring her to me in Zanzia. -King Dokar

Aurelia had very good handwriting. After giving the pigeon (this one she named Albert) a treat and securing it, she took out a piece of paper and wrote her own note, forging the king's signature at the bottom.

Good intel that Asha is no longer in Pome. Head to the Padua Mountains, find and secure the girl. I will meet you there. -King Dokar

She hoped this new message would help her sister.

In the days to come she intercepted three more pigeons headed to different locations, and to each she gave a different location for Asha, and a different location in which King Dokar was to be met.

The pigeons inward-bound were more difficult, because they were not part of the retraining process. She had to get to those birds before anyone else and switch the message before she was seen. With so little time to act, she pre-wrote messages to swap out. Her tree provided a clear view of the coop, allowing her quickly to make the exchange. These notes were essentially variations of the first one insisting Asha was not in Pome.

All she could do was hope she was doing the right thing. Aurelia was not used to having only herself to rely on. Asha and Rose had always been there to offer advice.

19

DAWN

It had been days since Asha last heard from Rowan and she could not sleep the night before he was to depart for Dumas. There was still the possibility that he would be waiting for her on the beach, and there was still that chance that she would go with him.

Would she really be turning her back on Zanzia if she went?

She was being hunted by an army. Honestly a ship voyage just might be the safest place for her. This might actually be the best thing for everyone right now, she reasoned. She was certainly not safe in Pome anymore.

And why shouldn't she have this one last adventure first? A chance to travel, to see the world, before she was committed to a stranger's kingdom forever?

She wanted to go.

But why hadn't she heard from Rowan?

And what if he wasn't on the beach when she went to meet him?

What if he was?

The Prince of the Diamond Islands, or whatever stupid prince she was supposed to marry, could wait, or be replaced. She would come back for Zanzia, but there was something she had to do for herself first.

In the dark hours between night and morning she wrote a note to Rose.

My dear sweet wonderful Rose,

Don't be terribly cross with me. I have decided to travel to Dumas with Rowan. I will be back soon, of course. I will still be the girl that saves Zanzia. But for this time, I will be hiding out where no one can find me. I will be safe. You are my best friend. I know I am disappointing you, but I do think it is ultimately for the best that I go. Until my return.

All my love,

Asha

Asha secured her itchy wig that made it look like her head was being used as an ostrich's nest. She briefly wondered how long she would have to wear it to keep up with charade of being Claire. Wearing it on top of her thick mane of hair was very uncomfortable. She packed a small bag. It was easy because she hadn't brought much to Pome to begin with. She crept her way outside the castle, deftly dodging the guards. In the end she had to jump from a high window ledge. Returning the same way would be impossible, but that didn't matter. She would not be going back. She crept slowly and concealed herself in the shadows. She moved at snail's pace to stay unnoticed, which also made her path out of the castle seem endless.

After what felt like an eternity Asha made it to the beach. She scanned the shore for Rowan, willing him to be there. It was still dark, though the moon cast long shadows and the ocean waves glowed in the moonlight. She finally caught sight of a silhouette watching the ebb and flow of the tide.

She began to run but caught herself, her soldier instincts kicking in. She was not yet close enough to be sure the silhouette belonged to Rowan.

Asha edged closer, cautiously. It had to be him, but she had to be sure. Finally, she was close enough to recognize the contours of his face. She let caution fly and flew across the sand, grinning broadly, yelling, "Rowan!"

She thought that at any moment he would turn and run to her. She was ready to leap into his arms. Her heart raced.

Rowan did turn to face her. He stayed put with his arms firmly crossed and his legs fixed on the shore. She pulled next to him, dropping her bag in the sand, stopping awkwardly. He appraised her without speaking or moving.

"Rowan?" she said, confused by his change in demeanor from all the times she had seen him before.

When he finally spoke his words were clipped. Formal. Cold.

"Claire. I'm happy you have come to see me off. I would have not wanted to leave without having a chance to say goodbye to you."

"Goodbye? But I thought ... I mean I had decided..." Asha managed to stammer; too confused to form a proper sentence.

"It was folly that I invited you, Claire. Frankly I don't think my fiancé would approve," Rowan said, his face slightly ashen.

"Fiancé?" Asha repeated dumbly. "You have a fiancé?"

Rowan replied with a curt silent nod.

"You are getting married," Asha stated. It wasn't a question. It was more like she was trying to explain the situation to herself.

He nodded again. Her mind was reeling. She searched for something to say. None of it made sense.

"You love her?" she asked in almost a whisper.

Rowan looked fully at her now, his eyes softening. "I do, I love her."

"And this is what you want. You want to be with her?"

"I want to be with her more than anything in the world," he said softly.

All the foolishness that led up to this ridiculous moment overcame her. Rowan's words had been an unexpected punch to her gut. Asha had questions, but none of the answers would be of any use to her now, so she bit them back. "Then you must go to her. You've certainly wasted enough of my time already. Go now." Her eyes blazed with anger and betrayal.

He didn't move and he didn't look away.

"I am so sorry, Claire." He did look sorry, but he did not look like he was changing his mind either.

"Go!" she barked. He gave her one last mournful look and he walked away, leaving only footprints in the moonlit sand. The tide was already erasing any sign that he ever existed at all.

Asha stayed at the beach for a long time, a frozen statue on the shoreline feeling so utterly foolish, until waves finally reached her, forcing her to pick up her bag and retreat.

She walked back to the castle, numb. Such a different journey than the one she had on the same road less than an hour before. Her feet seemed to move on their own accord, knowing the way so that she did not have to command them. Her hollowness throbbed.

Foolish girl! she told herself.

To think she had been willing to follow him. To think she had justified it to herself that such a voyage could keep her safe. Step after step she followed her feet to the castle, berating herself the entire way. She was not a worthy princess of Zanzia.

But she knew how she could fix this.

Arriving at the castle gate, she pulled off her wig and shoved it into the astonished hands of the guard on duty. Walking across the castle grounds, one by one she tore out the pins that kept her hair in place, discarding each with a ping on the cobblestones as she went.

She was done hiding behind a disguise. Done pretending.

She was the princess of Zanzia, after all.

When she reached Rose's chambers, Asha crawled into bed with her childhood companion. Rose put her arms around her and held her as she had done when they were smaller. Rose never asked why. But she could guess much of it, especially when the long blasts of a ship leaving harbor filled the air.

20

A NEW DAY

When Rose awoke, Asha was gone.

She shook herself awake, feeling worried. Had Asha left again? She put on her dressing gown and went in search. She stumbled sleepily into her mother's drawing room, and her mouth dropped open to see her dear friend as she had never seen her before.

"While you slept, we have been busy," remarked Rose's mother, pins in her mouth.

Indeed, they had. No less than a dozen maid's helpers rushed around the room, Asha at the center, resplendent in a golden gown with red and blue panels, embroidery, black piping, and a short train. Her hair was ornately gathered into a type of extravagant crown a foot tall and wrapped in Asha's long locks. She looked nothing like Asha, and everything like a princess.

Asha fixed her eyes on her friend. They were the only thing that gave her away. While all other aspects of Asha were magnificent and dazzling, her eyes were despondent. Her voice was chipper, but insincere.

"I've decided to marry the Prince of the Diamond Isles after all," she told Rose. "The choosing ceremony is today, and I had no proper clothing and no guardian to act as chaperone. Your mother has kindly offered her services. I can never thank you enough, Lady Marza."

"Nonsense child," said Rose's mother. "What is good for Zanzia is good for all of us. I think this will be a fine match. I just wish you had come to me sooner. It took us hours to comb out her hair!" she said, seeming to pin the criticism to Rose, as if hair combing had somehow been the most essential part of her duties to Asha. Asha shot Rose a small, secret smile to say she understood.

Rose wanted to argue with her friend. Asha never wanted to marry so young. It was a discussion they had many times, and the one thing Asha held on to. And the Diamond Islanders -- they were a greedy, militant race that had destroyed and pillaged their own land for the sake of wealth.

There was nothing good here for Asha. But Rose could see, as plain as Asha could, that they were out of options. Asha had resolved to sacrifice herself for her kingdom now, instead of waiting until she was older. They had run out of time. There was nothing left to be argued. It was a terrible decision, but it was the only one.

"Rose, the bath is drawn, your dress is hung on the bathroom door, and your sisters are waiting to do your hair. Quickly child!" said Lady Marza, sending her youngest daughter away. Rose suddenly felt a rush of gratitude for her mother and this place that she had never quite fit into. She was useless to Asha in this moment, but her mother knew exactly how to help.

Rose suddenly remembered something she could do. "Asha! Your mother gave me a letter and told me to give it to you, if you found yourself having to make any impossible decisions. A bit of motherly advice maybe. Do you want me to fetch it?"

"Yes, please. That is what I need more right now than anything else in the world!"

Asha read the letter from her mother. It carried the official stamp of Queen Kirsten of Zanzia in the corner.

Dear Asha,

If Rose gave you this letter then you are in the middle of making a monumental decision, and you must feel completely alone. Let me remind you that no matter what the future might hold, you are, at this moment, the crown princesses of Zanzia in line to take the throne. That gives you power.

You may find yourself having to go through negotiations without your father or me. You have full authority to do so. Both due to your status of ascendant to the throne, and because I trust you and grant you this right. You have learned everything you need to know, and you are old enough to use your knowledge to save Zanzia. I believe in you.

Whether you choose to go into hiding or to marry or to negotiate with the king of Nadroj himself, I trust you will be doing the right things for the right reasons and making good decisions. Trust yourself. Whatever is happening, just know you have prepared a lifetime for this moment, and let your instincts and training be your guide. I've included in here a sealed order permitting you to negotiate on my behalf. Use it however you need. My darling daughter, you are the last and best hope for our kingdom. I love you.

Mother

Included with the letter were the terms of the duel previously signed by King Dokar.

The letter gave Asha the resolve she needed.

21

THE CHOOSING CEREMONY

Her shoes hurt, and the dress made it hard to breathe. Asha could barely sit down in it. And the metal cage-like contraption sitting on the top of her head dug heavily into her scalp. Asha had never looked so beautiful – or felt so wretched.

She had felt a great relief and weight off her shoulders last night, when she had decided to marry the Diamond Isle Prince. But today this certainty seemed like a long shot. There were eleven other girls at this event, each looking more elegant than she did. The process had only just begun, and while the other girls seemed to know exactly what was going on and had their parents and great processions of people with them, all she had were Rose and Rose's mom, Lady Marza.

The choosing ceremony was taking place at an ornately built cathedral near the Pome Palace. But when the doors were opened to the ballroom where the event would take place, Asha was stopped by the official at the entryway. Lady Marza was not deemed important enough to act as Asha's guardian in the initial ceremony.

"I'm sorry," said the important acting man with the book, "according to the rules, your guardian must be of royal heritage, or a relative, and you say this is the mother to your lady-in-waiting?" It did sound rather unofficial when he put it that way, in his nasal voice.

"What can I do?" asked Asha, stricken at the now obvious error in judgment she had made.

"Nothing, I presume," the man replied, dismissively. "Be better prepared next time? Read the rules before you come? Better luck in the future." Asha felt the walls closing in. She didn't even want to get married, but this was her last chance to save her kingdom, and she couldn't even do that.

"Nonsense," Lady Marza exclaimed. "You wait right here, Asha. I will be right back." Rose's mom jumped into the carriage they had arrived in and ordered Rose to join her. They disappeared in a flurry of hoofbeats.

The minutes ticked by. The ceremony official kept sighing deeply and checking his time piece. Finally, he said that they could not wait for Lady Marza any longer and abruptly wished Asha goodbye.

The man slowly shut the heavy wooden doors, locking her out of the ballroom. She felt the same as when King Dokar had unexpectedly punched her in the stomach during their duel. Even if Lady Marza came back with a solution, it would be too late. It was over. As much as it should have been a relief, it was not.

This was the end for Zanzia.

Suddenly there was a bustle of bowing and "your majesty-ing" and in walked the regalest person Asha had ever seen in her life. Her gray hair was topped with an elegant crown, and her voluminous dress was complemented by a blue velvet cape. While Asha had not seen her before, she knew immediately who she was, the great Queen of Pome, one of the most important people in the world, and she was clearly not happy about being there.

The Queen of Pome marched up to the important man with the book. "What is the meaning of this!" the queen boomed, "I have had to leave my afternoon tea with the Duchess of Cantoon because you refuse to acknowledge the legitimacy of the Princess of Zanzia?"

"My greatest apologies, Your Majesty," whimpered the very important man. "Clearly your vouching for Princess Asha is more than sufficient."

"No, you dragged me all the way down here to participate in some ceremony. So, let us have it then."

In the next moment Asha found herself arm in arm with the famous Queen dowager, promenading through a stately room. Asha had no idea what she was doing, but the queen, despite her age, led her so gracefully and so forcefully that Asha could not have missed a step if she tried. She wanted to convey her gratitude to the Queen and tried to think of the right thing to say. Before she could get a word out, the Queen, without looking at her, said in a quiet voice that only she could hear.

"So, you really disarmed Dokar in front of his entire army? Hrump! That I would have given anything to have seen."

"Thank you, Your Majesty," said Asha. "It was pretty much the best moment of my life."

"You have more panache than any princess I've ever met. Never lose it."

And with that the princess was given a final twirl by the Queen, who abruptly turned on her heel and marched out of the room as her servants scurried to keep up with her.

Asha had been so focused on the Queen of Pome that she had failed to look around to see what her future husband might look like. She scanned the room for someone matching the description, but she could find no one who appeared to be a potential groom. Upon a more thorough examination of the room she noted a screened area to which everyone else in the room appeared to be directing their attention. The Diamond Isle royal family must be behind that screen, she thought. At first, she found this unsettling, the idea of being watched without being able to see back; being judged without being able to see who was judging. But upon reflection she realized that she would want the same if the roles were reversed, free to act disinterested, free from wearing fake smiles for all those girls and their families, eleven of which would ultimately be rejected. She was sure some of the other girls already had been but didn't know it yet.

Asha was in fact relieved not to have to lay eyes on her aging, fat, dripping in diamonds husband-to-be. She could get through this day, as long as she didn't have to look at him.

After the group session there were individual interviews, each of which dragged on endlessly, especially for Asha, who was called last to appear in front of the screen. At this point she had been standing for nearly nine hours, had not slept at all the night before, and was eager to get this charade behind her. Rose and Lady Marza followed her, several steps behind, as she walked into the room.

"Now announcing the Princess of Zanzia!"

Asha decided to forgo the initial pleasantries and launched into explaining her position, which she had been considering since the early morning.

"Good evening your majesties," she began. "Thank you for having me here today and forgive me for putting my name forward at the very last moment. I am Crown Princess Meliasha Esmerelda DeBurn of Zanzia. I come to you today because our kingdoms are in great need of one another. You have lost your lands. But you are a fierce nation with a formidable army. In Zanzia we have an abundance of land, but we are losing them to a northern threat. Our army is made up of starving farmers who cannot quell this tide. I am prepared to offer you a new homeland in exchange for its protection."

She made this offer with a lump in her throat. Had it come to this? Giving away part of Zanzia in order to save the rest? Part of her knew that this was always going to be the deal – her land and herself in exchange for an army to take on King Dokar's forces. They had to bargain with what they had, and they had so very little.

"We welcome you, Princess Meliasha," said a kind female voice from behind the screen. It was an older voice. Perhaps the queen? "Yours is indeed a very attractive offer and will require further negotiations. Who is here to negotiate on your behalf?"

"I negotiate for myself and on behalf of our kingdom. I have been authorized by my parents, the King and Queen of Zanzia. I have all the necessary documentation, if you desire to inspect it. Since along with our lands I am also offering up myself for marriage, I feel this is only right."

She spoke bravely to the center of the screen, not knowing where else to look.

"That is commendable, young princess. To be frank, this is the most appealing offer on the table. While I have many further questions for you, I recommend that you move immediately into negotiations with our constable Sven. Sven!" The important looking man with the book immediately rushed up.

"Thank you, Your Majesty," Asha said forcefully, "But I am offering up myself and part of my kingdom today. While I am certain Sven is a fine...constable, I will not negotiate with one who can only make decisions based on the rules in a book. Let me talk to someone who is actually empowered."

Sven looked stricken and insulted, and there was much whispering that ensued from behind the curtain. After a moment's pause there was a great rustling, and an older couple appeared from behind the screen. They had white hair and brown complexions and seemed to emanate kindness. Asha decided she liked them both immediately.

Sven bowed deeply and stepped to the side.

"Child," the old man said in a kindly voice, "I am King Adrien from the Marian Islands, and this is my wife Queen Takeisha." He noticed the confusion in Asha's face. "Oh, I see, you only know us as the Diamond Islanders, but that was never our name. Our beautiful islands were called the Marian Islands, named for the great love of our first king, his wife Queen Marian. We have much to talk about. Shall we sit?"

Asha answered him honestly. "I would love to, Your Highness, but unfortunately this dress prevents that."

The king looked at her thoughtfully. "I see. But seeing as this is the most important treaty negotiation of your life, and also ours, I'm afraid I must insist. I expect this to take some time, and you must be famished. I am certain we have more appropriate attire for this next stage of the process." He snapped his fingers and three ladies appeared. "Could you please find Her Royal Highness something more suitable to wear for head-of-state negotiations. And arrange for us to be brought our dinner in the drawing room."

"But ..." stammered Asha. "But what about all of the other princesses waiting to hear? We can't just leave them waiting."

"No," smiled the king, "Indeed we cannot, and this is why we have already sent them away."

Lady Marza gasped, and Rose put her hand over her mouth.

"You see my child," King Adrien continued. "As you have already recognized, our needs align very nicely. Had we known earlier that you would be joining us today, we would have likely dispensed with the selection ceremony altogether. Now, I will see you in the drawing room for dinner."

Asha was led away by the three ladies and trailed by Rose and Lady Marza in nothing less than a daze. She had done it!

Before leaving the room she turned back to King Adrien. "Your Majesties, will you have someone dispatch a pigeon to my parents letting them know?"

The king snapped his fingers again.

22

THE MARIAN ISLANDS

King Adrien was right. Three hours into talks, and the tables were spread with maps and dinner plates. Asha had brought Rose with her and between the two of them, their many years of tutoring and tedious hours of learning were paying off, along with their many trips together and a deep understanding of Zanzian lands. The document signed by King Dokar agreeing to honor the original borders was, according to Queen Takeisha, a very big deal.

"You hardly need us at all. All you need is for the international body to enforce this treaty," Queen Takeisha mused.

"Oh, if it were only that easy!" Asha said with a laugh.

Early into dinner it became apparent Asha and Rose knew less than nothing about the Marian Islands.

"Tell me what you have heard about my people and my lands," King Adrien asked of Asha.

Asha answered honestly. That she had heard they were a violent group that had mined their islands out of existence. "But I never tried to find out anything beyond the rumors and the gossip. I should have learned more on my own before I came here today. I deeply apologize for my lack of knowledge."

"No," King Adrien said, sadly. "It is not your fault. This is the message about us that has spread to most of the world. According to lore, we are greedy and violent and destructive. It was the excuse to chase us out of every place we ever dwelled. Let me tell you the real story, and if you will indulge an old man for just a little bit, I will start from the beginning.

And so, King Adrien told the tale of the Marian Islands

In the beginning, there were two brothers, twins, and the full story of these brothers is one for another time, but one was good and the other was not.

The nice brother, Benedict, was the older twin and was to be king of their country, though a rough and bitter country it was. The younger twin, Eustace, born only six minutes later, felt cheated of his birthright. Eustace grew up bitter, jealous, ever since he was old enough to understand by how little he had missed his chance to rule his kingdom. Eustace devised a plan to banish Benedict and steal the crown.

What Eustace didn't understand was just how clever his older brother was, and his plan played right into Benedict's plan to escape their cruel kingdom and start fresh in a new land. Benedict also had felt stifled from birth, but for different reasons. He despised how the people in his country valued brute strength over learning, power over kindness, fear over truth, and short-term selfish gains over the long-term prosperity of the kingdom and its inhabitants.

So, Eustace, in a plan he had thought was very clever, overthrew Benedict and banished his brother, along with 100 families who were sympathetic to the rightful king, exiling them to what we now call the Marian Islands. Eustace even signed over the islands to his brother officially, certain he was sentencing his brother to a doomed existence. The island was said to be an empty, unhospitable rock with poisonous waters and carnivorous land creatures. As a boy, ten years earlier, Benedict had been on an expedition to this island, and he himself played up, or even started these rumors as best he could. Benedict had befriended the local inhabitants on this trip, and learned of the island's secrets as well, and these he kept closely guarded.

Like I said, this is a long story, but the short of it was that once the families arrived, they found paradise. Far from undeveloped, the 100 families arrived to find that Benedict had been working for years on his plan to start afresh and had built each of them a home.

Once on the island, everyone was assigned an occupation, the thing they were good at and most passionate about, that was to be their job. A beautiful school was built, along with a hospital and a university. Benedict had encouraged everyone to bring books, and a great library had been built from tropical wood, carved with the curves of a conch spiral. Poverty and hunger did not exist in this land. The island itself appeared to be the source of the wealth, but the secret of that wealth was closely guarded. The people only knew that they were living this wonderful island life and wanted for nothing. Benedict chose his wife himself, a love match, the first in memory, and you already know her name, the good Queen Marian, who the islands were named after.

Things were good for a time, but for Eustace it was not enough to have stolen the crown from his brother and to preside over his stolen kingdom. Eustace heard about this mysterious island with its hidden source of wealth and wanted it for himself. And so, he came with a warship to attack his own brother. Benedict, who had foreseen so much and planned so well, had underestimated his brother's jealousy. It was a small peaceful island of mostly scholars and carpenters with many children, so Eustace would have surely succeeded except for one critical mistake. The ship needed fresh water. Some of Eustace's men snuck onto the island to get some. Now these were good people, and had they been asked, any one of the islands inhabitants would have surely directed the enemy away from the particular spring Eustace's men selected. It was full of bacteria and not at all safe to drink. There was indeed poisonous water on the island. The entire crew became horribly sick with dysentery, and thus had no chance of defeating the Marians, as they had come to call themselves.

But Benedict would not let this weakness remain. Now the king could see that while he might be able to keep the source of his great wealth a secret, the wealth itself was already known, so to protect his people he must teach them how to fight. And so, the island trained in the martial arts together, as one. Every morning at sunrise, the Marians would meet and train in combat. The island was rigged with cannons to dissuade any warships from coming near. There were more attempts to claim the Marian Islands, but none successful. And so, for hundreds of years three things about the island remained true: It was a paradise, every morning its people trained in combat together, and the prince or princess in line for the throne always picked a love match to marry.

We sent our children around the world to be educated, and we Marians had the brightest minds on this planet. And so, it was, when a bright student returned from a volcanic area of the world and told us our long dormant volcano was on the verge of waking up, we listened.

We evacuated everyone, nearly everyone. Not everyone considered the warning to be real. I was on the last ship with young Prince Magnus. He was only six. And so, we could only watch in horror when behind us our island erupted into an inferno that consumed our paradise. We had almost nothing but the clothing we wore and some limited sentimental items.

But our reputation for violence that we had carefully cultivated to keep us safe on the island preceded us, and we were rumored to have been so greedy to have caused our own demise. No one wanted to bring that violence or bad luck on themselves, and so they cast us out, time and again. After so many years we still remain homeless.

And after all these years, it appears we were just waiting for you, Princess Meliasha, to find us the home we have so long been yearning for.

"Please, call me Asha," she whispered, almost reverently. Asha was intrigued by this story, and her heart immediately went out to the Marians and what they had to overcome. She admonished herself for having known so little and having filled in the voids with nonsense.

"Your Majesty," Rose interjected, unable to contain herself. "You didn't mention the diamonds." Lady Marza shot her daughter a disapproving glower, making Rose slump down in her chair.

"Indeed, I did not," said King Adrien, nodding to Rose. "Of course you are curious, as you should be. The reason the secret to the island's wealth was so heavily guarded was that the diamonds themselves were relatively easy to retrieve. They simply lay on the ocean floor, created and spat out by an ancient underwater volcano. Diamonds as large as coconuts, just sitting there for the taking. A single one of these diamonds, as you might imagine, could pay for every need of every person in all of the Marion Islands for more than a year, and so we stockpiled the wealth across the world and invested the money, and over time these investments grew. The easy diamonds were collected a long time ago, and the only ones left were too deep to reach. The search for new diamonds became increasingly dangerous for our divers, and increasingly unnecessary, and so it had been more than

100 years since the last diamond dive when the volcano erupted."

"Yet here we remain," he said sadly. "A stranded people without a land, as petty rumors swirl around us.

"What happened to the Marians after the volcano?" Asha asked.

"In the years since we lost our lands, our people spread out across the kingdoms. We asked them to become scientists and architects, carpenters and craftsmen, doctors and teachers, soldiers and explorers, and to prepare to one day populate a new kingdom. All of our children are trained at the Marian Academy, the largest gathering of our people that we are allowed. We have passed on our language and our military training to our youth, which likely has not helped quell the world's impression of us. And now here we are, about to be saved by the most unlikely of heroes."

He paused for long enough that Asha realized he was expecting her to say something.

"Oh, you mean me? I am not your hero, your Majesty," she admitted. "I believe you are mine."

"Then it seems we have both found what we were looking for. I believe we are going to make a very good team."

After many hours a plan began to emerge. The Marians would be given a large swath of land encompassing all of the "disputed lands" that Nadroj had stolen. The same lands Nadroj continued to threaten as they slowly crept the border forward over the span of several decades. While the coastal areas would go back to Zanzia (she had seen that to lose the coast could mean loss of access to trading routes, and she simply could not lose them again) there was an island off the coast of these lands that would go to the Marians.

"To have an island, no matter how small, you don't know what this means to us," said Queen Takisha.

The Marians would also be given a significant piece of land in what was now considered the "northern border." It broke Asha's heart to be giving away this land, the place where she had spent so many nights under the stars and racing her horse against Rose's.

Until she realized, abruptly, that quite apart from losing it all of it, this would be her new land, the land that she would be queen over, someday, after marrying the Marian Prince. It would be the New Kingdom of Marian, and she would be its queen.

She changed tactics and began to creep the border forward, but only slightly, and curve it to include a secret cave, a favorite waterfall, and a hidden glen. She wasn't giving these places away; she was keeping them for herself. Her anxiety began to subside.

Yet here she was, carving up her kingdom, marrying a stranger she still hadn't met, at only thirteen. It was everything she never wanted. She just had to remind herself over and over again what and whom she was doing it for.

23

THOUGHTS OF A KING

Back in Zanzia the situation was growing more dire. King Dokar had initially expected his stay to remain brief in the hopes he'd acquire "that girl," as he referred to Asha. However, the reports from the field were muddied and elusive, and he felt no closer to capturing and marrying the idiotic princess than when he first arrived.

A long standoff had not been considered, and so everyone, including himself, continued to pretend he was a visiting dignitary. He had no better plan, and that in and of itself made him grumpy.

Queen Kirsten and King Henrick did what they could to entertain him, first with cards. He enjoyed playing, initially, until he started to suspect King Henrick was letting him win, after which Dokar refused to play. Now, night after night, he was serenaded with strumming guitars, dancing maids, ancient fiddlers, and Zanzian poetry. It was enough to make him lose his mind! He decided when all of this was over every last performing Zanzian would be thrown into the dungeons to make up for him having to endure being among their audience.

The accommodations, despite being in the castle, were musty and uncomfortable. The mattress was lumpy, the sheets were rough, the tapestries hung to make the stone walls look brighter had seen better days (and perhaps better centuries). The only decent food available was what he brought in after breaking the embargo, and because it was supposed to be a state visit rather than an invasion, this meant he had to share all of this fare with his hosts and have it cooked in their kitchens. The looks on the faces of those Zanzians! He began to wonder how long they had survived on potato mash. He had no intention of ever eating another plate of tasteless mush.

He complained bitterly, and to everyone. But there was very little to be said in response to his endless rants.

It was he who had painstakingly, and with full intent, created every one of these hardships that he was now personally having to bear. From the old linens, the cold of the castle, the lack of decent food and drink, even the lack of servants. In a way, King Dokar reminded himself, the degeneration of Zanzia was just a testament to his success. He remembered what his poor, crazy father had told him once, during one of the mad king's more lucid days.

"I have tasted success my son...and it tastes bitter and vile." The old man had then laughed hysterically as two of his aides came to take him back to his chamber. But those words had always stayed with Dokar, and he thought of them now.

King Dokar couldn't stand another day emersed in the abject poverty of Zanzia. It was time to dispense with this foolish farce and head back to Nadroj. He would have to imprison Zanzia's royal family first, of course. Perhaps he could still use them to lure *that girl* out of hiding. He suspected Asha was far away now, with not a single credible report or sighting.

If keeping King Henrick and Queen Kirsten didn't help him to capture the princess, he would simply kill them. He'd make a public spectacle of their hangings. Something to show the Zanzians *he* was their ruler now. The royal family seemed so weak and passive, two traits he despised. He wondered if anyone would even interfere when the time came. He had less than a dozen men with him, and the so-called Zanzian "army" was still stationed at the northern front. What fools. He should have taken over their country years ago, he realized now. This was all going to be too easy.

Maybe he would keep the younger daughter. He could use someone to play cards with, after all. And while she was not nearly full grown and not a first born, she would come of age in time. A wicked smile crept across his face as he considered this new plan. It reeked of progress, and action. He felt satisfaction now, looking around, knowing this would be one of the last days of having to stay in this forsaken place.

24

HANGING IN A TREE

Hiding in the tree awaiting pigeons was good for Aurelia for two reasons; she could interfere with the messages, which was her main goal, but it also allowed her to watch the comings and goings of the Nadrojian soldiers while staying safely hidden.

She didn't like how they eyed her hungrily, as if she was a prize that might be plucked in the absence of her sister. So far, the soldiers had participated in the polite charade of their king, but Aurelia was nervous that the false niceties would end abruptly, and she felt safer being out of the way where she could observe. The problem was, if a pigeon did arrive, she had to burst from her sanctuary in order to intercept the message – which was announced loudly by the clanging of a bell – voiding all of her protection in an effort to ensure the safety of her kingdom.

This time she spotted the pigeon before it landed. She hurried to the coop, hoping to arrive before the bell rang. She dropped from the tree without making a sound and raced to the coop. The path was fast and direct, and allowed her to stay out of sight, though it did require some climbing. She raced up the remaining steps of the wooden platform where the coops were, hearing the flutter of wings. She had only one small platform to cross!

She lunged for the bird but it was too late. The pigeon was just outside her grasp and entered the cage, causing the bell to ring.

Aurelia snatched the message attached to its leg, quickly replacing it with another she had prewritten. She wasn't sure which replacement note she had grabbed. Nor did she have time to read the incoming message.

Heavy footsteps approached from below the coop. She dashed to the rail. One quick flip over it and she could safely escape. But for the second time that day she was too slow. Strong hands grabbed her, pulling her back, jeering.

"One princess, just as the king ordered," said a soldier, who stood taller than the other accompanying him.

"We've been looking for you!" said the other with the red mustache. "You haven't been exactly easy to find. And trying to steal the messages from the pigeons have you? Looks like we caught you red handed!"

"No-no," Aurelia managed to stutter, "I was only greeting them. And you came running up the stairs and scared me! I didn't even read the message. See, it is attached." She wasn't sure if she was a good liar, so it felt safer to stick to things that were true, even when being deceitful.

"We don't actually care about the pigeons, do we. We are under orders to bring you to the king," said the taller soldier, menacingly.

Aurelia pulled away. "No. My father would have never sent you for me. You are lying!" She said this ferociously in order to stall.

But she didn't feel ferocious at all. These fully-grown men man-handling her in her own castle frightened her tremendously. If they thought they could get away with this, and here of all places, then a great shift had already occurred in Zanzia.

Seemingly in response to her unspoken fears, the mustached soldier picked her up as if she was a ragdoll and slung her over his shoulder. "Your daddy ain't the king anymore, sugar. King Dokar, he's the one that wants you."

She pounded on his back, and screamed and writhed, but it was all to no avail. The soldiers only laughed with amusement, and no one came to her aid.

The guards had talked casually as they carried her through the castle, and down into its bowels.

"So, do you think he is going to hang the whole lot of them?"

"I'm not sure about this one. King Dokar may want to keep the girl. She might come in useful later."

"What a sight, eh! The royal family hanging from their own royal trees in their own royal yard."

"I wonder how long he'll toy with them."

"Only until he grows bored."

"A couple days then?"

"I reckon so."

Finally Aurelia was dumped unceremoniously onto the dungeon floor deep below the castle. Her parents were already there, and she flung herself into their arms. The relief at being reunited with her parents flickered only for a moment, as she realized the gravity of what this all meant. Zanzia's royal family were now captives in their own prison.

The day that all of Zanzia had pushed against for so many dark years was now upon them. King Dokar had quietly taken over the entire kingdom. Not incrementally from the North, where a cold and hungry army of farmers remained to try and stifle his advances, but here, within their own castle walls, disguised as guests. How silly it seemed now to think that Asha could wed the right man and somehow all of this could have been prevented. Sitting on the cold stone floor, which oozed its own supply of dank, frigid air, this ending seemed inescapable and inevitable.

Aurelia wasn't sure what she feared more – death by public hanging, or to be kept alive and used as a tyrant's plaything. If it came down to it she would die bravely. She would never serve King Dokar.

Queen Kirsten held her daughter close and stroked her hair. When Aurelia tried to speak, the queen shushed her, and pointed to the guard. "Wait until he sleeps," she mouthed.

Hours later Aurelia was surprised to see her favorite Zanzian servants approach their cell. She brightened to see Orrin.

"I've brought you some after dinner tea, sir," the servant said politely to King Dokar's man guarding their cell. Aurelia gasped, seeing that Orrin had not come for the royal family.

"Orrin! For shame!" shouted Aurelia, tears pricking her eyes. "How can you serve the enemy?" Orrin kept his eyes downcast but could not hide his shame.

"I am but a servant. I serve this castle and its rulers."

"We are the rulers!" said Aurelia, weeping openly now. "What about us?"

"I serve whomever is in charge, Your Highness." Orrin said, as he hurriedly retreated up the stairs, after bowing to the guard.

Aurelia saw for certain that no one would be coming to save them.

25

PRINCE OF THE DIAMOND ISLANDS

Asha pulled uncomfortably at the neckline of her dress. It was two nights before her wedding, and tonight was the night she was going to meet her husband-to-be. She felt like she was about to throw up.

Her parents had not arrived, which really was too much to ask since the pigeon had only been sent the day before. Rose sat rigidly beside her, aware of her friend's deep unhappiness. The silence weighed between them.

"Can I get you a glass of water?' asked Rose.

"Oh, Rose." Asha was not feeling like being the center of a ball in her honor. "I know why I have to marry him, but why do I have to meet him tonight? If I meet him and I hate him, I don't know that I will be able to go through with the wedding, and I know that I must."

"You really should just get it over with. He can't be so terrible. After meeting him you might even look forward to the wedding!" That comment received a ferocious look from Asha.

"I can tell them that you are not well," Rose said, more a question than a statement.

"I am not well," decided Asha, "and I'm not going. Quick, get me out of this!" She turned her back to Rose, indicating the hundreds of intricate buttons from neck to hem that needed to be undone to release her from the fabric prison that was her gown.

Asha slipped into comfortable pajamas and was sipping hot tea by the fire when Rose returned from cancelling the first meeting between the betrothed. She wore a look on her face that Asha could not discern.

"Tell me ... did you meet him?" asked Asha, raising an eyebrow. "Was he as awful as we imagined?"

"I did not meet him. Actually, when I got there, they told me it was good I came to cancel, because the prince also was not feeling well. His family had been about to cancel dinner as well."

"What? He doesn't want to meet me?" It shouldn't matter to Asha, but it did.

"Asha! You are impossible!" scolded Rose. "You are the one who cancelled on him. The poor prince probably is *actually* sick."

Asha discovered a new possibility. The prince was not just a stranger she would be forced to wed, but one who had no interest in marrying her either. For tonight, she had delayed the end of her childhood, but the fate that had hung around her neck like a noose since the day she was born. She had only one more night of freedom after tonight, and she wished she could enjoy her final days, but try as she might, she could not.

26

THE KEY TO EVERYTHING

It wasn't long before the guard nodded off. Aurelia, who had already resigned herself to the end, was surprised to see her parents spring into action as soon as the soldier's head slumped.

"Don't worry, my love," said Queen Kirsten calmly, kissing her youngest daughter on the top of her head.

She removed a key from a chain around her neck and brushed away some straw scattered across the floor. There was very little light, but Aurelia could see an indentation.

Her mother inserted the key into a lock. A portion of the floor creaked open.

Aurelia was sure that the guard would awaken when the stones groaned apart, but he didn't stir. Her father went through the trapdoor first.

"Jump and I'll catch you," King Henrick said before disappearing into the darkness.

How could he see her, let alone catch her? The images in her mind of what would happen if she stayed in the cell felt like a noose around her neck. She had to trust in her parents' plan, and dropped into the utter blackness.

Just when she thought she would hit the ground, or worse – fall forever – her father caught her, just as he promised. Her mother came last, and together her parents quietly closed the door and re-engaged the lock. The queen placed the key back around her neck.

The dank, enclosed area was pitched into complete darkness. The air was cold and heavy, like a stale tomb. Aurelia's father took her hand, and her mother placed a hand on her shoulder, and they walked along slowly, but with seeming confidence. Aurelia couldn't tell if it was authentic confidence, or simply put on to comfort her.

They stumbled along for a very long time, until the king finally stopped. They'd reached a solid stone wall. "The key, my love," he whispered, and Kirsten fumbled in the darkness. Aurelia imagined that if her father dropped the key it would go skittering off into the blackness and into one of the many cracks and small crevices they had been walking over. They would be trapped here forever. Better than the gallows, she thought. But the king did not drop the key. The wall opened, letting in the light of the moon, and they tumbled out into the once familiar backside of the castle garden.

Aurelia was shocked to see Orrin standing there, a man she just recently regarded as the enemy, and she was even more surprised to see her mother run to embrace him. The queen laughed at her daughter's confusion.

"You provided fantastic cover for me, Your Highness," Orrin told Aurelia, grinning widely at her.

Understanding dawned on her. "You put something in his tea!"

"Yes, well, we had to make sure he slept soundly so you could get away. I wasn't sure he would trust it coming from me, but your outburst was perfect." He tousled her hair.

Aurelia threw her arms around the old servant.

The relief was short-lived. King Henrick spoke in a hushed voice "We are not safe here. Orrin, what is the next plan?"

"I am short on information, Your Majesty," said Orrin. "I am not clear on the best next course of action."

There was a pensive silence as the adults looked at each other, until Aurelia finally remembered what she was carrying in her pocket.

"I intercepted a pigeon!" she practically yelped, handing over the rolled-up note to her father. It had been too dark in the dungeon to try and read it, and she hadn't wanted to say anything earlier for fear of being overheard by the guard. They waited in anticipation as the king first read the note to himself.

It could be anything. It could be nothing. Aurelia only hoped it was useful.

When he had finished reading the note, Aurelia's father handed the note to her mother. "It is from King Adrien from the Marian Islands. Although he says we might know him better as the King of the Diamond Islands. He says that Asha and his son are to be married on Tuesday morning, and that we should come if we can."

Everyone began talking at once.

Queen Kirsten: "We have prayed for this for so long."

Orrin: "And now we are long on information. A much better situation indeed."

Aurelia: "Oh no! I heard that the Diamond Island prince was old, fat and mean! She isn't really going to marry him, is she?"

King Henrick: "Tuesday morning is too soon. The horses will not be fast enough, and we cannot ride in the open."

Because time was of the essence and they needed to move quickly, the topic of transportation was the one that broke through.

Other than horses, there was only one way to the wedding and it was exceedingly dangerous. There was the Lords Terror River, but it was so violent – constant rapids and white water – that few used it for travel. No one with better options, at least.

Too many of King Dokar's men would be on the roads, and even if they were lucky enough to avoid them, they would never make it in time for the wedding. The river might kill them, but they had already escaped death once tonight.

There was one final issue, and that was leaving the castle and all of Zanzia in the hands of a murderous usurper.

"If only I had called back the troops from the northern border," bemoaned King Henrick. "I had thought Dokar's presence in our castle was meant as a diversion from the northern front. I even sent Max up to the front to oversee the battle. I know it is not really an army, but they do have the numbers to protect our people from King Dokar and his handful of men. Since I did not, and since I cannot leave my kingdom in a madman's hands, I must stay." He looked very sorrowful as he said it, as if staying now would be the last thing he might ever do.

"Um, papa?" said Aurelia. "Remember when I told you that I've been intercepting the pigeons? Well ... I might have also sent a note telling the northern troops to come home. I wanted them here to protect all of us!"

It had only been after she had sent the pigeon that she realized how big of an overreach of authority she had made – impersonating her father to dictate troop movements. She was pretty sure this constituted treason. But since she had been doing it already with Dokar's troops, she hadn't thought. She just did it.

And since then she had been dreading the moment that she was going to have to tell her parents what she did.

But rather than scold her, her father swooped her up into his arms. "Oh, you clever girl!" he said as he deposited her on his back. Aurelia's act decided it.

They would travel the Lords Terror River.

27

LORDS TERROR

A battered boat had been stored near the river, in case of emergency. Since no need for the boat had come in many years, it had deteriorated, and now was weathered and peeling. Orrin checked on it once a year or so, fixing any leaks to ensure if would float if it had to. Unfortunately, one of the oars could not be located.

The river, illuminated by the moonlight, spat white spray as it charged down its path. It roared and swayed and looked like it would chew up the old boat with little effort, and the royal family with it.

"Are we sure this is a good idea?" asked Queen Kirsten, again.

It most certainly was not a good idea, but there were no good ideas left, or even mediocre ones, and so this was the final option that retained the slight possibility that it would save all of their lives (if it didn't also kill them) and deliver them on time for Asha's wedding (if they were not unceremoniously dumped in the river along the way).

Orrin decided he would stay behind. With the northern troops on their way back to the capital, he needed to intercept them and share everything he knew. But before that he would go back into the castle and try to sneak out as many castle staff as he could. It shouldn't be too hard, as there were not all that many of them left these days, and Orrin knew all the secret ways in and out of the castle. The ones that Aurelia liked to think of as her own.

The family of three trepidatiously tottered into the unstable vessel, while Orrin held on tight to keep them steady, and gently pushed it from the shore. It reminded Aurelia of a time she'd gone sledding in the deep of winter. Asha and Rose had been holding the sled for her at the top of a steep hill while Aurelia climbed in. They let go, and the sled went careening down the mountain with a mind of its own.

Released, they shot down the river, immediately went sideways and nearly flipped, but King Henrick was able to steady the boat with the single oar. Once straightened, the boat went rocking forward, riding the churn. The darkness made the difficult journey seemingly impossible. Aurelia held on for dear life, her mother constantly moving, trying to balance the boat, while her father worked the single oar in the darkness of the rapids. The boat danced into the waves.

Down, down the river they went. Every turn seemed surely to be the last. The boat flung itself forward into the night like a blindman's slingshot, fast and unlikely to hit its target. Aurelia kept her teeth clenched together to stop herself from screaming. Was it only hours ago she was to would die by hanging? Now she was certain she would drown. There were many near misses over the next several hours. Waves broke over the sides, drenching them in freezing splashes. Mother and daughter bailed furiously with their shoes, both infuriatingly ineffective and dangerous because they could only hold onto the boat with one hand.

A wave caught the boat and tossed Aurelia overboard. The queen caught her by the foot and dragged her back in again. They each lost their bailing shoe in the process, but resolutely took off the other and began to bail again.

Dawn rose over the river. They could see each other better now: wet, shivering, barefoot, but alive. They couldn't stop for a moment. Oaring, bailing, steadying, bracing, holding on. It was a gruesome ride with no end. Their bodies ached from the cold and from the effort, but it seemed like they had finally found the rhythm of the river.

Hours rolled by, unnoticed and unmarked. The river sped up again. Too late, numbed by lack of sleep and repetition, they understood why.

A waterfall loomed up ahead.

It was too late to ditch the boat and try to swim to safety. The roaring of the river grew. They could only hold on to each other as they were flung over the edge, hurtling them to certain demise.

28

REVERSE EXODUS

In preparation for the wedding, Asha and Rose had left the castle of Pome and were now guests of the Marians, staying in a cozy cottage. The wedding was to take place on a plantation outside of Pome, and a bit closer to Zanzia. The girls sat on the top stairs of the house in which they were staying. It was the day before the wedding, and they watched an endless stream of travelers arrive. These were the Marians (not the Diamond Islanders, as she had to keep reminding herself). They came from all corners of the globe, called by their king to the wedding they had spent half a generation waiting for.

Asha watched them as they came in, including the children born after their homeland dissolved in a fire of lava. She watched elders, being helped along, who would have already been old on the day that they left their homeland by boat, expecting to return shortly.

They came, not in the dress of their original island home, but in the clothing of their adopted lands. Beautiful women dressed in so many different styles and colors. Their dark hair long and short, in elaborate up-dos, and down and casual. Men in sarongs, suits, and everything in between. They came from farms and cities, palaces and country pastures. The girls were mesmerized watching the progression. The arriving Marians did not seem to quite know who they were yet, so the girls were able to just sit in relative anonymity on the porch, in a lovely patch of sun, drinking iced tea and eating fried egg sandwiches provided by a servant.

Asha wondered about the Marians, and about the lives they had built up over more than a decade. These were her new citizens, finally on a journey to come home to a place they had never before seen. What would they think of their new land? Islanders that would now have to live in landlocked mountains. They were refugees who had been unwelcome in every place they went before. They had learned new languages, paid for their groceries in unfamiliar currencies, dressed in foreign clothing, but no matter how hard they worked to fit in, their children had been ostracized, and they had been met with fear, disgust and distrust regardless of where they traveled.

There was good she could do here. She could offer these unlucky islanders a place in which they would never again feel like they were an outsider. It would be hard work creating a kingdom out of the wilderness – especially one that replaced sunny sandy shores with winter snows and rugged peaks, but she would work alongside them. She would learn their language and their traditions. If she was to be their queen, she would be a good queen, she would do that at least.

The steady flow of visitors continued as Asha and Rose finished their tea. Despite her watchful vigilance, she never found the faces she most longed for – her mother, her father, her sister. She knew they couldn't possibly travel such a long journey and on such short notice. It had taken she and Rose three days when they fled to Pome, and at that time they moved as though the devil were chasing them.

The pigeon carrying the wedding invitation had only been sent the day before, and yet it worried her that there had been no reply. She had in fact only heard from her family once, the message that Aurelia had sent.

Her mind developed worst case scenarios in which they were captured or dead at the hands of the Nadroji king. She hoped that against all odds they would arrive before the wedding. Her sacrifice seemed only meaningful when surrounded by the light of her family.

29

THE HARD WAY

Aurelia broke through the surface of the lake, gasping until she had enough air in her lungs to scream. She was entirely alone. She scanned in every direction and saw no one. Where were her parents?

"Mama! Papa!" She was sobbing as she bobbed in the cold, expansive lake.

"I'm here child, shhh, it's okay, it's alright. We all made it." Queen Kirsten's arms were suddenly around her, and King Henrick was doggie paddling over to his wife and daughter.

The waterfall had, thankfully, thrown them clear of the debris and dangerous churning that could have fatally trapped them underwater at the base of the waterfall. They swam to shore, muscles cold and stiff from being crouched so long in the boat and their limbs not wanting to function correctly. At least it was now dawn and they could see.

Once onshore they gathered wood and built a fire. Devoid of nearly all of their belongings, Queen Kirsten managed to still have a bit of flint deep in a pocket. Soon all of their clothing were steaming. The Queen refused to let them move from their spot until everything was toasty and dry. As they spread out their soaking garments to be dried, they even discovered a small fish that had gotten inadvertently captured in the folds of the queen's cape. They skewered it and shared the tiny meal.

"I just remembered something very important Orrin told me," King Henrick said to his family.

"What was it?" Aurelia asked.

"He said whatever you do, make sure to take the boat to shore well before reaching the waterfall." His eyes were apologetic. Queen Kirsten laughed out loud.

Their eyes rose to the steep slope up the cliff they had just come over.

"Well, good thing you forgot that bit of advice. It would have been quite difficult climbing down," said the queen with a wink, making Aurelia laugh too.

None of their shoes has survived the encounter with the waterfall. The trio was exhausted and battered from their journey down the river. They staggered through the woods, trying to find anything resembling a path or trail. Something that might lead to a road.

Barefoot, dirty, torn robes. Aurelia wondered if there was a royal family anywhere in the world resembling the three of them.

The brush was dense and fought them every step. Aurelia's father led them toward a distant mountain. He hoped it was near the plantation where the wedding was to take place.

For hours they trekked. With very little indication they were actually making any progress getting anywhere at all, they suddenly stumbled out onto a road.

The king was sure that this back road saw very little use, but at least the going would be easier. But no sooner had he mentioned this than a carriage passed, and then another. The riders were singing and festive and the next carriage stopped immediately, even though they must have looked like road-side vagabonds.

"Excuse me, are you lost?" a woman with kind eyes asked them. "Do you need a ride?" The King and Queen smiled at each other, then at Aurelia.

"A ride would be most welcome," said the King.

The family couldn't believe their luck, and were further delighted to learn that the carriages, and many like them, were all headed to the wedding. These were the Marians being called back to their king and queen.

The owners of the carriage were exceptionally surprised to learn that they had just picked up the royal family of Zanzia, the mother, father, and sister of the bride on the way to the big event. It was now past midday, and they would not arrive until long after dark. After talking with their carriage mates, having a hot drink and a lunch of cold chicken and chunks of aged cheese, King Henrick, Queen Kirsten, and Princess Aurelia snuggled up together in the back of the swaying carriage, and promptly fell asleep.

30

REUNION

Asha lay in bed, while Rose slept next to her. In the morning she was to be married. She stared resolutely and blankly ahead. Sleep was out of the question. For her at least.

Asha only hoped that her act would indeed save her kingdom of Zanzia. Otherwise it would all be for naught and she would still be trapped. So much sacrifice for so little guarantee her sacrifice would be worthwhile.

Her thoughts strayed to Rowan. The boy she had liked and lost, all in a flicker. She would let herself think of him this one last time. Then never again. He seemed like a distant dream already. She let herself imagine, just for a moment, an alternative life. If he had been who she thought he was, if she had gone with him on a ship, escaping across an ocean. The consequences would have been devastating – both for the Zanzians and the Marians. But she pictured herself with him, on the deck of a ship sailing to Dumas, together as they watched islands and fishing boats pass as they voyaged on. She could almost feel the wind in their hair and the sun on their faces. Her heart ached over everything tomorrow promised.

Suddenly there was a pounding at her door.

She opened it to find her mother, father and sister. Each had a blanket wrapped over their shoulders, and they were scratched, disheveled, dirty, barefoot, and very much worse for wear. But they embraced her as though their lives depended on it, laughing with joy to see her.

"I was certain something had happened to all of you!" said Asha, unable to hold back tears as she hugged each and every one of them. "I worried you'd been captured ... or..."

"We were captured, by King Dokar," said Aurelia, proudly. "But Mama had a key, and Orrin poisoned a guard, and then Papa led us over a waterfall and ..."

"Hush now," said the King, giving his youngest daughter a wink. "Everything worked out perfectly, did it not?"

"Come in and tell me everything!" said Asha.

As servants brought in fresh clothing, food, a warm pot of water to soak their feet in, Asha's family told their harrowing tale of escape. Asha and Rose told of the choosing ceremony, and of carving up their kingdom during the negotiations. Despite it being late, and her parents being exhausted, her father wanted to know every detail of the treaty that had been negotiated between the two kingdoms. Her father listened and nodded, as Asha and Rose laid out what had been agreed.

Finally, at the end of the presentation, he sat back in his chair, and nodded.

"It is a good deal for both nations. They give us protection and will help with the work to reclaim the land that has been taken. In the end, they get a homeland, and we get to have an end to our decades-long conflict with Nadroj. You have done very well Asha and Rose." Rose flushed to be included in the praise. She had not expected it.

Before the servants finally led her parents and sister away to hot baths and clean beds, her mother took Asha aside.

"Tomorrow comes too soon for you, I know daughter, but for Zanzia tomorrow may have been too late already. You are saving all of us Asha, and I am so incredibly proud of you!"

Asha had met the Marians, and now her mother was here. She would hold her head high tomorrow. She would marry for her kingdom, with pride.

31

DAY OF RECKONING

It was the day of her arranged marriage. Or, as Asha had always considered it, her day of sale.

Since as long as she could remember, she had thought of this day as the end of her life. It was the day she had dreaded since she was six years old, the day she had tried to avoid with all her might, but it had come even sooner than she feared.

However, her anger and despair had left. She had already accepted all of it.

A union between the Marians and the Zanzians could bring peace and a better life to so many people. Such a noble act gave her solace, but that sure didn't mean she was happy about it.

Asha prepared for her wedding. Servants had been sent in to do her hair and help her dress in wedding fineries. The

Marian kingdom had provided her with a beautiful wedding gown and a diamond studded tiara. The tiara was crafted to represent the ocean waves the Marians loved so much. Despite her unhappiness with the day, Asha found it breathtaking. Asha was also relieved to discover that her dress was actually comfortable, and she could even sit down in it. She considered her refection in the mirror the servants had set up for her. Aside from the scowl on her face, even she had to admit she looked perfect, which made her scowl even more.

Her family came and went throughout the morning, as did Rose. Gone were the somber, understanding faces of yesterday. Now everyone was downright giddy, and it was infuriating her. She had continued to mentally prepare for the ceremony as one might prepare for a battle.

She was a 13-year-old bride dressed up in adult clothing in order to save not one, but two nations full of beautiful people. She was marrying a man, whom as far as she could tell was as unenthusiastic about marrying her as she was about him. This should be a somber affair. But still everyone's faces shone with grins and sparkling eyes.

She glared at Rose, who only laughed back. She hugged her sister fiercely, only to have Aurelia dance merrily out of her grasp. Her mother beamed at her. Even her father was borderline giddy. There was simply too much gaiety and joy for such an occasion. Wedding fever had infected everyone but her.

Asha felt so alone and isolated in the midst of all of her favorite people. Now that it was finally here, she willed this day to be over. She could no longer bear the anticipation of this unwelcome day.

Asha put on her veil. It was lovely and soft and thick, and she could hide her emotions beneath it. She wondered how long she could wear it for. A day? A year? Forever?

She was told it would be a very long aisle. Thousands of Marians would be there, having been invited weeks before, even in the absence of a selected bride. Many dignitaries from other lands were also expected. For some, her promenade down the aisle would be all they'd see of the wedding.

Finally, the music began. Her father, with only a slight limp to show for his trials from the day before, escorted her by the arm. They exited the farmhouse onto the path that would lead her to matrimony. Although she had been told to expect a crowd of onlookers, her jaw still dropped in awe.

There were so many people! The Marians had come to the wedding – the wedding that would allow them to no longer be immigrants – in mass and were spread out as far as she could see. Asha thought about all of the other Marians who must still be on their way with all of their worldly possessions, ready to build a new kingdom. In all directions, she could see more streaming in. On horses, in carriages, on foot. It was an exodus in reverse, and though she wanted to cry, it was beautiful.

They smiled warmly as she passed. There was an air of merriment surrounding them, and without realizing it Asha's hardened grimace faded. It would be too much to say she smiled, but she could not entirely resist the contagious joy of the crowd either.

As she walked up the aisle, through the sea of people, she noticed a handful of Zanzians, though they were outnumbered thousands to one. Everyone was standing, so she could never see very far ahead. Coming around one bend, Asha saw the Queen of Pome with several of her ladies in waiting, including Rose's mom. She gave a deep curtsey in her direction, and the old monarch gave Asha a wink in return, which helped steel her resolve. She had to be getting close to the end!

Around every corner, she had braced herself to finally lay eyes on the groom who had equally been forced into this ridiculous arrangement. Finally, there he was in front of her.

What she saw made her stop in her tracks, and gasp.

Her father let go of her arm and even took a few steps back, dissolving away from her. She did not have time to process this. Her heart leaped and dropped within her chest. She tore off her veil. The rest of the world disappeared.

There, standing in front of her was a very familiar figure. One she had thought of so often in these last few weeks. There, looking anywhere but down the aisle at her was her very own Rowan.

"Rowan?" She must have shouted because her voice carried, and he turned and looked back at her, his eyes growing immeasurably wide. She thought he might be cold, like he was the last time that she had seen him on the beach, but his face registered so many emotions at once. He ran to her, stopping short as he seemed to take in the thousands of eyes upon them.

"Claire?" he said, stunned. "Why are you here? You aren't supposed to be here. What are you doing here?"

"I'm getting...married," she said, as confused as he. None of this made any sense. "I ... I thought you were engaged?" she stuttered, as it was the first thing that came into her head.

"I was ... I mean ... I am. But apparently, I am ... I mean I was ... engaged to you?"

A sea of understanding washed down on her. "Wait, *YOU* are the Prince of the Diamond ... I meant the Marian Prince?" She shook her head to clear it. "So, who are you, actually?"

Rowan eyes widened as he put all of this together. He beamed at her.

"My parents, they made me give you up. But they made me give you up for *you*!" The prince's expression turned from confusion to elation. "This is beyond bizarre. I'm so confused right now!"

Rowan closed the distance between them, threw his arms around Asha and twirled her around as she hugged him back tighter than she'd ever hugged someone before.

The crowd twittered and oohed.

Rowan put her back down and pulled away from the embrace, apprehensively. "I have to know something first. Do you even want to marry me?"

"Well, I was expecting something much worse!" Asha blurted out. "I mean, I'm so happy it's you. I can't believe that it's you! I really didn't expect to get this lucky."

"But you don't actually want to marry me now, I think. Because, my dearest Claire – or whoever you are – I might not know your name, but I remember everything you ever said to me. Today, I know that you are a soldier going off to battle. You argued quite persuasively that royals should not be married until they are adults." He gazed into her eyes compassionately.

"I didn't want to be forced to marry at so young an age, it's true. But Rowan ... you. I just don't know what to call you!" Asha sputtered to a stop, realizing she wasn't even sure she knew his name.

Without another word he kissed her. Right there, in front of everyone. Long before anyone had said you-may-kiss-the-bride.

They kissed and the whole world tilted away. She could feel the kiss all the way down to her toes. The crowd roared their approval. They were on their feet, clapping and stomping and whistling.

He finally pulled away and whispered, "So, your name is Meliasha then?"

"Call me Asha," she replied, barely regaining her voice.

"Asha," he said. He looked at her, his mind calculating something. "Do you trust me?"

"I mean, I think so?" Asha replied honestly.

"And you negotiated the treaty, right? Between our two countries. Is it a good agreement? You like it?"

"I do," she said, this time with confidence. "It is a good agreement for both of our people."

"And your family wants to implement the terms of the agreement immediately?"

"I'm not sure what you are asking," she whispered back. "But we all agreed that the treaty must be ratified without delay," she said, falling back into the language of the contracts and governance.

He took her hands in his. "Good," he said. "Then we are agreed."

Agreed to what exactly, Asha was not sure. She had missed a clue to something in their conversation, that much was clear.

Before she could put the pieces together, he got down on one knee, still holding her hand in his. "Will you marry me?"

"Yes!" Asha yelped, blushing, but very confused, as she was quite sure this had already been established. She was wearing a wedding dress after all, and standing not very far away from a minister and an altar.

The prince got up slowly, still holding her hand, but now he looked outwardly at the crowd that had been leaning in silently, trying to hear the exchange between them.

"I have an announcement to make!" he yelled, hushing the assembled crowd. "Princess Meliasha and I are getting married!"

The crowd whooped and hollered in approval, and someone shouted, "We know!" to much laughter.

"But we are not getting married today," he continued. The crowd was silent as a confused murmur moved through the assemblage. Asha was confused along with them. Were they not getting married?

The prince winked at Asha. "We will be married one day, once we are all grown up. In the New Kingdom of Marian!"

All the crowd needed to hear was the words the "New Kingdom of Marian." They cheered and applauded wildly. The Prince had to wait some time before it was quiet enough for him to speak again.

"As you know," the Prince, formerly known to Asha as Rowan, continued, "the Marians marry for love, and the royal heir gets to choose who they wed." He paused. "And you are going to have to wait years before the real royal wedding, but I *choose* Asha!"

The crowd roared again, more wildly than before.

"Despite no wedding today, the treaty between our two kingdoms has been sanctioned and will still go into effect immediately! Today is not my wedding day, but it **is** the beginning of New Marian! Great people of Marian, you have been long on patience. You have sacrificed and suffered, you have been in purgatory all of these years, but no more. Tomorrow, we are going home! But tonight, we celebrate!"

His words were met with thunderous applause.

People began getting up from their seats. There was nothing more to say.

The wedding was over before it had even begun.

Asha just stood there, stunned and smiling. She had been so caught in the moment, she suddenly remembered that her family was there, and looked for them. She saw them in the crowd, with her younger sister, clapping wildly with the rest of the Marian crowd. Tears streamed down her mother's cheeks. Aurelia jumped up and down, unable to contain herself. Rose beamed with a familiar smirk Asha knew all too well.

"You knew?" she mouthed to Rose, who nodded vigorously. Of course Rose knew. At some point she must have seen the prince and recognized him as Rowan. It must have been why Rose had been so happy this morning. She knew how Asha felt about Rowan. Rose had clearly told Asha's parents, and even his parents. King Adrien and Queen Takeisha nodded at Asha with wet eyes and brilliant smiles from near the alter. Everybody knew. Except for her and ...

Asha turned back to the prince. "Magnus. Is that your name?" she asked.

"Yes," he said.

"Hi!" she said back, awkwardly, as they both grinned at each other.

They both had so many questions for each other. But it was impossible to talk about anything now. They were swept away in waves of well-wishers and dignitaries. Rowan – no, Magnus – rooted himself by Asha's side as the crowd ushered them toward the ball that was meant to celebrate the wedding. Asha grabbed his hand, unwilling to be parted, and also to prove to herself that he was truly real, and not just a dream that would sail off once she awoke.

Asha had been wrong about today. It was not to be an ending. Only a beginning. The beginning of everything.

After much dancing, food and merriment, everyone settled in for one last night of luxury and peace and Asha said good-night to Magnus.

"So, Magnus" (she still couldn't get used to him being Magnus instead of Rowan) "what do you actually know about book binding?" Asha inquired, as she tried to reconcile the prince standing in front of her to the boy she had come to know.

"Well, I do like to read," Magnus conceded with a chuckle. "And I've always been curious about octopus ink. And that's pretty much it." Asha laughed.

"So how do you feel being engaged instead of married?" he asked.

"Well, I rather like being the fiancé that you left me for," laughed Asha. "And I really like not being married. I know it sounds strange, but that was pretty much the best wedding gift you could have given me today."

"It doesn't sound strange at all to me," Magnus replied.

Asha stayed awake for a long time, in the room she shared with her parents and her sister, despite not sleeping much the night before. Had only a day passed since she had felt like her life was over. She now felt as though she was on the precipice of the life she had always wanted.

32

JOURNEY TO THE PROMISED LAND

In the morning the entire column of Marian and Zanzian wedding guests and revelers had transformed into pilgrims and warriors, as they set out for Zanzia. They did not have thousands of horses, and so they walked.

Asha was offered a horse but it seemed silly.

She could not arrive early and face off against King Dokar and his men without an army at her back (although she was tempted to try). And by no means did she want to slowly ride on a horse for days and days on end. She walked with her people, new and old, hand-in-hand with Magnus.

The horses were primarily used to supply the massive group. Thousands of meals needed to be prepared twice per day, and so the horses went back and forth, bringing ingredient and firewood to the cooks and servants, then distributing meals to the people. The Marians all carried their own plates, cups, and serving utensils, Asha learned, along with a great many other things.

It was a strange procession. Asha knew they were going off to war, but the experience was more that of a giant walking celebration. Magnus introduced her to an endless array of people, many of whom he had clearly not seen in ages. Every single one had a story. Every single one seemed relieved that after so many years of living in exile and unwelcome, that they were finally coming home. To their new home.

Asha and Magnus talked about the monumental task they had facing them.

Building a kingdom in the wilderness with no roads or infrastructure would be difficult in its own right, but these lands first had to be wrested away from the clutches of the Nadrojians who had laid a false claim to it. Bloodshed and dark days seemed inevitable. But no one seemed deterred. On the contrary, all were giddy and grateful to the Zanzians. The caravan of travelers continued on, slowly marking the miles on their way to a new kingdom.

As dark as the days to come were expected to be, Asha and Magnus found solace and beauty during the long days of walking, hand in hand. At night they camped on the side of the road, which stretched out for miles.

Asha finally asked Magnus about what had happened that morning on the beach, and why he never replied to her letter in the wall.

"I was caught! I was putting a letter to you in the wall. Are you sure you want to hear the whole story?" Magnus asked. "It was deeply humiliating actually, but you may find it entertaining."

"So, I may have gone a bit overboard in my affection in what I wrote," he admitted shyly, "I had written about running away with you and everything. And out of nowhere, constable Sven shows up. How do I explain Sven to you?" Magnus mused. Asha remembered the man who had tried to keep her out of the choosing ceremony.

"Oh, no explanation needed. Sven and I have our own special history. Go on," she told him, eager to hear this story.

"So, Sven takes the letter from the wall and reads it. He then said that due to the traitorous content of the letter – that was his word for me, *traitorous* – he was declaring me an enemy of the state and said that gave him the authority to make a house arrest. He escorted me back to my parents, and insisted on reading the letter, out loud, in front of them. I was mortified. My dad was kind about it, but explained again, as if I hadn't heard it before, the long struggle of my people, and how I am the only hope for salvation. So of course, I am convinced that I have to go through with the arranged marriage." Magnus relayed this to Asha as part comedy, part tragedy. Asha found herself laughing out loud in spite of herself.

"And it turned out to be good you did," said Asha with a laugh. "Maybe I'll have to be a little more charitable when I think about Sven in the future."

"To be honest," he went on, "the real reason I agreed to it, was that I thought about what **you** had said, at the Bookcase Café. That marrying for one's country impacts thousands of lives and is the most noble and selfless act there is. The 'nation's fiercest warrior' you had said. And of course, I knew my parents were right, and you were right, and everyone was right but me, and I made the only decision left to me.

"But I couldn't stand the idea of never seeing you again. So, I somehow think it will be a good idea to meet you on the beach, like we planned, but it was terrible! It was such a bad idea. The way you looked at me. I didn't think I could feel worse about it until that moment. And there was nothing I could do or say. They made me promise to only say goodbye to you, and not give you a clue as to who I really was."

"But then you ended up with me anyhow," said Asha smiling. "And you didn't even have to get married!"

"That really is your favorite part isn't?" Magnus teased Asha. "Not marrying me?"

"I mean, when you put it that way..." replied Asha with a twinkle in her eye.

Asha noticed every Marian carried one of the long wooden staffs similar to the one that Magnus always carried. The rods clipped into a steel spike on one end, and the Marians pushed the spikes into the ground. They carried lengths of fabric in each of their bags, and they attached these to the tops of the poles, creating a massive tent-like structure that kept out the dew and kept in the warmth, even though they were sleeping on the ground. An entire kingdom cuddled up together under an enormously long and colorful tent roof.

The beauty of the patchwork of colors in every direction as far as she could see took Asha's breath away. The idea that all the Marians needed was for a few good friends to join them, and with these materials they would always have a home – no matter where they were – warmed her heart. She was falling in love with these people, who someday would be her people.

Magnus gave Asha a funny look.

"What?" she retorted.

"Well, of all the things that are new about you now that you are Asha and not Claire, there is just one thing that I am having trouble getting over." His eyes shifted upward. "Your hair."

"My hair? You don't like my hair?"

"Well, no, it's beautiful. It's just very...well-manicured, and very...long. It is just not exactly the hair I imagined for the warrior princess of Zanzia, that's all."

Asha gave Magnus the side-eye at that remark. "Oh, I like it! It's not criticism. Please don't take it the wrong way. I had just gotten used to your *other* hair."

"Well, thank goodness for that," Asha smirked.

Before anyone could stop her, Asha gathered her hair over her right shoulder and hacked at it with her sword.

"I didn't mean you should cut it!" said Magnus, aghast.

"Oh, believe me, this is not for you," said Asha, still sawing away with her blade.

She sliced through the last of it and stood triumphant, heavy, long train of perfect long blond hair in one hand and sword in the other. She shook her head, glad to finally be free of all the weight she had carried since she was a young child.

"Now, there's my girl!" said Magnus, laughing and shaking his head at her.

"I do feel much more like myself now," she grinned back.

Day after day they walked. The longer it took, the more the joy drained from Asha. What had become of Zanzia in the absence of her family? A knot formed in her stomach to think that the Zanzians had been abandoned to the whims of King Dokar and his men. Images of flames and burning houses danced unwelcomed in her imagination.

Her entire life had been manipulated in order to keep her people safe from the northern king, and yet here she was with the entire royal family, a several days journey from Zanzia with the vengeful Dokar in residence in their castle. How much destruction could he reap before they arrived?

Aurelia told Asha of how she had confused his troops by planting false messages on the pigeons. At the first telling Asha had marveled over the heroicness of her sister, but now she was filled with doubt. How much could a little girl and a few birds really do in the face of an evil empire? King Dokar's entire army was probably in Zanzia by now, going house to house and rounding up the villagers.

At night she dreamed that all of the homes of the Zanzians had been set on fire, and everyone was screaming for Asha to save them – but no matter how hard she tried in her dream, she could not get to them fast enough, and they perished before her, screaming her name.

She willed the massive column of people to pick up the pace. The children and elderly who would not be part of the battle and moved most slowly were not part of this first group. Still, the progress seemed tediously slow. Magnus walked with her, and listened to her concerns, but they were doing the best they could. They were an army of thousands and would soon arrive in force. But that did little to assuage Asha's guilt and concern.

Finally, they camped just miles from the border. They would arrive in the morning! Asha could not sleep for the dread of what they'd find. The lump in her gut pierced like a twisting stab wound. She lay awake in the darkness of thousands of sleeping warriors, all too far away to yet be of any help. After several hours of sleeplessness, Aurelia tumbled into her from the dark beyond.

"Asha," she whispered, breathless and panicked. "I snuck out and rode to the castle ... to make sure it was okay!" She was crying so hard she could barely speak.

"Aurelia, slow down and tell me what happened." Even not knowing what Aurelia would say yet, Asha was already getting up and packing her bag. There would be no sleep for her tonight. That was clear.

"I got close to the castle ... I wanted to see what was happening." Aurelia's words tumbled out. "And it was Orrin! He was ... he was ... hanging there!"

"What?!" Asha was alarmed. "Orrin? He's ... dead?"

Aurelia waved her hands. "No! He's alive! He's been strung up in the yard. He's battered and bloody and has a gag over his mouth, but he's alive. He saw me Asha. He looked right at me! I wanted to cut him down, but I'm not big enough and I didn't have a sword. Only my bow, and I couldn't do it with that. But I don't think he'll stay alive much longer. We have to go now!"

Asha surveyed the sleeping cavalcade and decided that if she started to wake people up one of two things was likely to happen. Either they would prevent her from going, or they would insist she wait for a large contingent to prepare to ride with her. After so many days of being forced to go slowly, she chose Orrin and action over waiting.

She wanted to tell Magnus, who was sleeping further away from her this night. But he also might try to stop her.

Asha tiptoed away with her sister and they saddled up two supply horses and left the camp. Between the road they were leaving, and the castle was thick, dense woods. Even if they made good time it would be hours before they'd reach Orrin.

The pre-dawn light began to let the girls see distant shapes in the darkness of the forest, but it was slow going as they picked their way along the rarely-used trail. Again, the slowness of the pace felt agonizing. Every branch reached out to smash her in the face, and each root did its best to trip the horses. Asha realized the horses were a mistake, and she would have made better time on foot. The brush was just too thick, but she didn't want to abandon the horses in the woods either, and so they pressed on. Finally, they reached the end of the forest where they could look out and see the castle.

In the shadows of the early morning they could see what Aurelia had described. A figure strung up on a wooden beam outside the walls of the castle. It was too far away to tell who it was, but Asha could see him move slightly. She felt terribly for the miserable man.

There were no signs of guards, no sign that anyone was awake except for she, her sister and Orrin. Asha and Aurelia snuck unnoticed across the castle grounds using the darkness that remained. Soon the daylight would betray them and expose any attempt at escape.

"Aurelia, I am going to quickly go over and cut him down and bring him back here. I need you to stay here. You can't help me, and I need to know that you are safe."

Aurelia nodded dutifully at her older sister. Asha, sword at her side, darted out into the open area, clinging to the shadows where she could, rushing to beat the blood-red of dawn washing over the yard.

No one blocked her way. Indeed, she didn't hear a sound.

She reached Orrin. His eyes focused on her face and he became frantic, hacking out indistinguishable words through his gag.

Asha climbed up the wooden beam, quickly cut Orrin free and helped him to the ground.

Her family's faithful servant tore off the cloth binding his tongue.

"It's a trap, Asha! I was put here as a trap. Run! Don't worry about me, just run as fast as you can!"

But it was too late.

33

SURRENDER

King Dokar confidently strode toward them across the lawn, and he was not alone. He dragged Aurelia with him, sword to her neck. Asha cursed herself. She had been so focused on Orrin she hadn't noticed what was happening behind her.

"My darling Asha, how lovely of you to come. And you even brought an extra *treat* for me," he said, motioning toward her sister with his blade. "How very generous of you."

"Leave my sister alone," hissed Asha, trying to sound braver than she felt. "You don't want her. You want me, and I'm right here. Let her go!"

Dokar laughed. "I want you more, it's true, but now I don't even have to choose. I get to have both. I set a little bitty trap and caught both of you in it. It is my lucky day. Now I hope you are feeling festive, because you and I are going to have a quick wedding before heading back to Nadroj." He added snidely, "Pity about the hair, truly. The wedding portrait will be simply ruined."

The blood left Asha's face. A marriage with King Dokar would nullify the agreements she had with the Marians. It would be the ruin of Zanzia and the end of the dream of a New Marian. She cursed herself for coming alone, and for bringing her little sister along.

She tried to think of what to say. "My sincerest apologies, Your Majesty," Asha spat back at him. "But as of recent I have a husband. You should congratulate me."

"You think I didn't hear about your sham of a wedding? It wasn't exactly a private affair, was it?" drawled Dokar. "You invited a couple thousand wedding guests yet didn't think I would hear that it ended without a wedding. My spies are everywhere. Of course this was very happy news for me indeed, my dear bride to be," the king gleefully said in return.

Asha scowled. "But I shall never agree to marry you, so it doesn't really matter now does it." Asha was biding for time. She needed to come up with a plan, a plan she did not yet have.

"Oh, but I can be very convincing!" King Dokar mused. "Especially when you brought your little sister right to me as a pawn. This really is a very simple negotiation process. Marry me - or she dies, right now." He paused. "And then you die."

He circled Asha like a shark waiting for the proper moment to strike.

"Luckily for me I am the one holding all the cards! Perhaps your parents told you of how they taught me to play games these last weeks. I was a quick learner. I think the right expression here is checkmate, dear Asha. Now, quick to the ceremony. Time is a wasting. The servant and your sister will be your wedding party. All I need is a minister, a few I do's, and we will be on our way to your new kingdom. My beloved." Asha hated how he lingered on those last words while eying her hungrily.

Asha had two problems in front of her. Her sister's life, and her own matrimony. Perhaps she could separate them and save one. "Okay, you've persuaded me. Let my sister go and I will marry you." At least she had to get Aurelia to safety.

Aurelia caught Asha's eye and moved closer to King Dokar. It made it more difficult for Dokar to keep his sword directly under her neck. But he did not appear to notice the small movement. His attention was on Asha.

Aurelia had Asha's attention, though, but Asha didn't understand what her little sister was trying to tell her.

"Forgive me if I do not *trust* you, my betrothed," King Dokar sneered. "In negotiations, it is always best to have an insurance policy, and I will be keeping mine."

"You have my full attention now, Your Majesty," said Asha. "Tell me what my life will be like as your queen. If you can persuade me that our union will be what is best for my people I will gladly comply."

Aurelia moved again ever so slightly. Asha was not yet sure what her little sister was doing, but at this point her little sister's plan was all she had.

"*Gladly comply*!?" scoffed Dokar. "We both know you will not gladly comply, Asha. But I will settle with *quickly comply*. My minister is waiting for both of us right now inside the..." as he gestured toward the castle, Aurelia made her move.

She dropped like a stone, out of his grip and sprung backwards, away from the king. He swung at her with his sword but Asha was ready. She deftly blocked his blade with her own, protecting Aurelia, as steel sang against steel in the morning air.

"Aurelia, run!" she screamed. Her sister took off like a rabbit toward the tree line.

The king looked equally amused and annoyed. "Guard!" he yelled out, without any urgency. A man in armor appeared from around the side of the castle wall. "Please retrieve the little girl for me, and if you can't bring her back in one piece, that is just fine with me."

That was not okay with Asha, and she attacked, as if that would keep her sister safe.

She rained down blows on Dokar, but her anger made her clumsy, and this time he was ready for her. He deflected her swipes with little effort, as Asha tried to attack the king while she willed her sister to move faster. Aurelia had a head start, but the guard took off at a sizable man-sized pace. Asha's heart dropped as she saw how rapidly he was erasing her sister's lead.

"And now you are just handing me the only other thing I wanted today," the king said in his bemused expression. "A chance to destroy you with my sword, as I should have done during our first meeting."

Asha couldn't concentrate on her swordplay. Her mind was on her sister. Aurelia wasn't going to make it. She was close to the tree line but the guard was closing in. He would overtake her any moment.

She nearly missed some easy blocks. King Dokar had control over the fight and was enjoying his advantage immeasurably. "Oh, what is the matter, dear Asha? Not actually a good fighter except for that one silly trick?"

He slashed with fury, and she again barely blocked. The tip of his sword caught her shoulder. She cried out in surprise. The blood instantly began to run down her arm.

Asha wanted to look towards her sister. She knew the guard must have caught up with her by now, and hoped he was not being too rough with her. She wanted to look, to make sure, but the second she looked away from the king, he would finish her. Her heart was breaking. She had to see! But she kept her eyes on Dokar instead, bracing for his next attack.

Instead it was King Dokar who lost focus on their battle. His attention was pulled by something. Rather than press her advantage in the fight, Asha turned to where she had last seen Aurelia running. Except the scene had changed.

Aurelia was still running. The guard was still running after her.

But now there were three additional figures in the field. The trio had clearly just emerged from the trees. Two men and a woman. Each was equidistant apart and were – in unison – twirling a Marian staff in a motion that was so fast that the weapons themselves were a blur.

Despite the fluidly of the motion, the movement also felt quite savage and violent. They halted the rods for the briefest possibly moment, allowing Aurelia to dart in between them, to safety, before setting their weapons upon the guard who had attempted to follow the girl. It was three against one and their staffs took him down nearly instantly.

The middle figure looked away from the guard and directly at Asha. It was Magnus! Of course it was Magnus. He glanced over at her with concern.

But there was nothing to be concerned about. Asha smiled at him across that vast distance, hoping he could understand her expression, and set about changing the cadence of the fight before her. The terror for her sister's well-being had left her paralyzed. Now she felt her strength returning, along with all those years of hard, practiced training. She trained her smile on the king, swinging her sword in fluid strong arcs, back on the offense, instead of the defense. The king took a tentative step back, giving her ground, but unwillingly, teeth gritted, grunting.

The fight belonged to Asha. She released an onslaught of blows, drawing blood from both of Dokar's arms. He yielded even more ground to her.

But then, both king and Asha were distracted a second time.

Magnus and the other two fighters continued to move forward. But now, out of the woods behind them emerged a second line of Marians, each moving in unison, each with their staff in motion. This line was at least 20 people strong. Behind them emerged a row of 50 warriors, all twirling their Marian staffs. Asha could see more Marians emerging from the woods higher up. Every row was followed by an even larger number of Marians, walking onto the battlefield, equally spaced. All moved in a practiced regiment of an army moving as one.

Magnus cried out in a language and a voice that Asha did not recognize. "KOM HË!" he yelled to his people. His voice carried across the field. As one, his people responded in a chorus that was part primal cry, part song, but unmistakably the rhythmic chant of a warrior tribe. The staffs continued to whirl, but now there were more motions. The voices ceased, replaced by the synchronized smacking of staffs. Magnus's people moved together as a singular force.

He called to his people again. "KAM HÂ!" The response this time was more complicated and melodic, but ferocious. Asha was mesmerized and somewhat terrified.

The bemused, annoyed expression that King Dokar had worn for most of their encounter vanished, and Asha thought she detected a flicker of fear on his face, perhaps for the first time. That flicker disappeared as quickly as it came.

"How quaint," he drawled, recovering his self-assurance. "Little boys and little girls with sticks. WHERE IS MY ARMY?!" Dokar bellowed.

On cue, a rumble began from behind the castle that Asha could feel in her feet. Soldiers on horseback galloped from where they had been waiting out of sight. Dokar and his men had clearly reclaimed the horses briefly taken by the Zanzians. The glee of victory that Asha had so briefly felt of was tampered back down, and suddenly she was petrified.

Dokar's army lacked the grace and discipline of the Marians, but they raged forward, possessed with madness. And unlike the Marians, every last one of them had horses. And armor. And swords.

The polished steel of so many hundreds of swords gleamed in the morning sun, blinding Asha. Her hopes for a peaceful Zanzia and a new Marian Kingdom plummeted. She was not yet queen, and already she had led her people to their slaughter.

As the Nadrojian army thundered by her, Asha remembered the day that she had seen them first. Dokar's soldiers were formidable. She knew that her own army of farm hands stood no chance against them. While the Marians might put up more of a fight, they seemed to be vastly ill-equipped to take on such an army. Their wooden sticks would be sliced into pieces. The horses gave the Nadrojians speed and height, leaving the Marians defenseless with no shields. Asha steeled herself for carnage. She blamed herself.

The Marians themselves did not appear deterred, however, and ran out to meet the Nadrojian army. She watched in horror as the Marians raced toward certain death. But as they ran, the numbers of those emerging from the woods never ceased. The Marian forces soon had the Nadrojians outnumbered. Yet their front line looked so exposed and vulnerable.

Asha locked eyes again with Magnus, worried this would be the last time she'd see him alive. He was positioned at the front of his army. If she had only waited, they could have formulated a plan. Instead Magnus would be the first to suffer the consequences of her rashness. She stepped in his direction.

Suddenly King Dokar swung at her full force, aiming for her neck. It was all Asha could do to drop and tumble in time to miss the blade. Dokar's strategy had changed significantly. He was no longer trying to best her in order take her home to be his wife. He was trying to eliminate her.

She let go of the battle forming around her. She was not about to allow King Dokar to regain an advantage. She raised her sword and pressed forward.

As Asha parried and exchanged blows with the king, the two armies collided. Asha could feel the reverberation shaking the ground and the violent sound hit her a second later. Magnus was surely gone. Was there any hope he could have survived? She could not turn to know for certain, and so she gritted her teeth, and channeled all of her rage into her sword and directed it at Dokar.

Asha needn't worry about the Marians. They were formidable and could take care of themselves. While the staffs they carried weren't forged in steel, they were crafted of Lignum vitae, the densest of hardwoods. What the staffs lacked in sharpness they made up for with reach. And, as Asha would have realized if she had a chance to reflect on it, the staffs were outfitted with steel spikes that had been used to transform the staffs of the Marians into a tent city at night. These were six-foot long solid rods with five-inch metal spikes affixed to either end. The staffs were deadly and could inflict a great deal of harm.

The Marians had something else too. They wanted it more.

The Marians were fighting for a home they had lived without for so long. Like Asha, they had each begun training at the youngest possible age, practicing every morning for a lifetime. The Nadrojian army was motivated by fear of a volatile despot.

King Dokar had built an army of soldiers fueled by fear, designed to never best him. The Marians pushed for each person in their landless nation to excel above and beyond every other so that together they might rise up one day as a force that exceeded the sum of its parts. Today was that day.

By swinging their staffs deftly and with brute force, the Marians separated the riders from their steeds and quickly began to take control of the horses. Throwing off the injured riders, Marians mounted the horses and attacked the Nadroji soldiers still on horseback.

Clearly this was a scenario the Marians seemed to be prepared for. Still, it was shocking to watch an army on foot with no swords or amour begin to outmaneuver a well-armed cavalry.

But Asha didn't see any of this, as a circle of Marians had closed around her, protecting her, but at the same time giving her enough space to continue and complete her fight. A circle of Marians, evenly spaced, staffs held out in front of them motionless, but ready to be engaged at any moment. Magnus was part of this group. Asha caught sight of him. Relief flooded over her, almost causing her to collapse, but her heart steadied. A second circle of Marians stood back to back with the first, staffs whirling, protecting the first circle. Magnus was safe. He was here ready to protect her, but also flanked and shielded on every side by those ready to protect him.

Asha understood what they were doing. The Marians were protecting their king and queen to be, but they also understood that this was her fight. They would not interfere unless they needed to. Their apparent confidence in her lifted her own self-confidence, and with her fear for Magnus now abated, Asha could finally turn her attention to finishing what she had started. And she had already decided how she was going to do it.

Asha smiled at the king. It was a gritty, raw smile, and then she ran at him full speed, sword clenched in both hands. She hit him as hard as she could. Dokar blocked, but the force of her blow sent him careening backwards. She was no longer trying to win this fight; she was trying to end it.

"My entire life I have spent living in your shadow!" she said, addressing Dokar, raining blow after blow down upon him. He was cowering now, barely deflecting her onslaught.

"The only solution that anyone could think of to save my kingdom from you was to SELL ME to the highest bidder to some kingdom far away. I learned this when I was SIX!"

Her voice changed from anger to triumph as she regained the advantage in the fight. "I won't be sold! You can't have my kingdom! And I won't ever again live in the shade of your cruelty! I am Asha! These are my people – Zanzians AND Marians. And you, King Dokar, are finished!"

Asha used all of her might on an upward blow focused on the grip of Dokar's sword. His blade slipped through his sweaty, bloodied hands and flew into the air. Magnus caught it victoriously, raising it up to the cheering of the crowd.

Dokar dropped to his knees. "Finish it then," he demanded, furiously, seething with indignity.

"You will have no such luck on this day." She swung at his head, rotating the blade at the last moment so it struck him firmly on his temple. King Dokar crumpled to the ground.

News that the Nadroji king had fallen traveled quickly among his ranks. His army, realizing they were outnumbered and outdone quickly began to surrender.

34

THE FINAL SURPRISE

It took most of the rest of the day to get enough supplies to the Zanzian capital to prepare a feast for thousands, but feast they did. The Zanzians came tentatively out of their homes (which, to Asha's relief, had not been burned,) and off of their farms to see for themselves that the Nadrojian army had indeed been defeated.

The Zanzians had given up on ever expelling Dokar's army and had already been resigned to a permanent occupation. Orrin had indeed spread the word of Asha's marriage, giving some hope, but in recent days the good people of Zanzia had been terrorized and traumatized by King Dokar's men, and felt that it was surely too late for a solution by matrimony. So, they arrived at the castle grounds elated. Reborn into a new story that could have a happy ending.

Everyone, the Zanzians and the Marians alike (and even many of the Nadrojians), were eager to retell the story of

Asha's sword fight with the king. Nearly everyone claimed to have witnessed his defeat with their own eyes.

The Zanzians were understandably uncertain about the Marians. They too had heard of the ferocious Diamond Islanders. But soon the word spread that they were not a second invasion but would take over the very northern reaches of Zanzia, along with all of the lands the Nadrojians had formally claimed, with the exception of the coastal lands.

All the Zanzians needed to hear was the fact that they would never have to leave their families to guard the Northern front ever again. The Zanzians hugged the Marians in gratitude. And the Marians hugged the Zanzians with even more gratitude, and soon everyone was hugging and laughing and crying with happiness and relief. It was the biggest party either nation had ever known.

Asha, for her part, never left Magnus's side. The royal pair gazed with pride and love into each other's eyes. Asha had liked Rowan, the book binder. And Magnus had liked Claire, the messenger. But they each found the real Asha and Magnus even better by a mile.

While Asha said she wanted Aurelia to stay by her side, she did not actually notice when her sister slipped away and into the crowd. Aurelia was a celebrity in her own right. Word of her deeds also spread across the kingdom. She paraded happily on people's shoulders, not only being given credit for her work scuffling communications, but also, and for the very first time publicly, being heralded as Zanzia's next queen.

Even the captured Nadrojians were allowed to join in the festivities. They had been offered a very good deal in exchange for their obedience. They could work for two years building new roads for the two kingdoms. If they worked hard, they would be paid for their second year, and permitted to go home during the third, as long as they behaved.

As for King Dokar, he was locked away in an underground dungeon, with no hope for release. While there may have been grounds to petition for his release under other circumstance, too many people had seen him swing his blade directly at Asha's neck. He had been charged with attempted assassination of a royal by two kingdoms.

As the festivities wore on, someone called from the crowd. "Who is to rule Nadroj next with the king gone? He has no heir!"

Asha too wondered what would happen in Nadroj. Their rules were clear about succession, which is why the kingdom had gone to a madman, the father of Dokar, when King Nret had died. The crown would sit on the head of the next heir, and King Dokar had no remaining kin. Asha saw her parents exchange a significant look with each other.

King Henrick got up to speak, and the crowd hushed.

"Good people of Marian, Zanzia, and Nadroj. I have information that will interest and impact all of you."

Asha had thought the danger from the north was over, and now she suddenly realized that of course there would be someone taking Dokar's place, and that the protracted conflict could continue into the reign of the next leader. She squeezed Magnus's hand.

"You are wondering who will lead Nadroj now that King Dokar is sentenced to life imprisonment, and thus loses the rights to his throne." King Henrick continued, "The succession rules in Nadroj are this: the crown must go to the eldest child of King Dokar, but as you know, he has no children. Next in line to the throne would be Dokar's siblings, or their offspring. But of course, Dokar was an only child. Finally, the rules mandate, his aunts or uncles, or their children, would be next in line. The great King Nret had two other children, in addition to Dokar's father. His younger sister Lady Mary died in childbirth, along with her child. Dokar had a brother, Constantine, who was much younger. Constantine died fifteen years ago. With no recognized heir within this line, Dokar was free to choose his own successor. He has chosen Commander Blackwell, of his personal guard."

Some frantic whispers and groans filtered through the crowd. Commander Blackwell was known for his ruthless and cruel nature and made King Dokar look like a charming man by way of comparison. Asha wondered if that was the point, as long as Dokar had named Blackwell as his next in line, then people would rally behind Dokar as the preferred king. This was disastrous news, she thought. They had taken down a king, only to have a second, ghastlier version take his place. She did not like this at all and took Rose's hand in her other hand to both calm and gain comfort from her friend. Indeed, three nations assembled here today were all to be deeply impacted. Her father spoke again, and everyone shushed to hear him.

"But unknown to most is that King Nret's brother Constantine did indeed have a child!"

The crowd broke out in rumblings and whispering. This would mean that Constantine's child would be the next monarch. Asha had never heard of an heir to Constantine. Would this be more bad news?

It took a moment to hush the crowd before King Henrick could speak again. "Constantine's child was hidden, and yet raised with a formal royal education. The truth was hidden from everyone, even from this child. This child will be the next ruler of Nadroj and will be a phenomenal leader and ruler!"

Everyone talked at once. Who could this mystery person be? Asha wondered who her father would call phenomenal. How would he even know this hidden heir?

King Henrick remained at the pulpit, and a person from the crowd moved to join him. Not the person Asha expected. "Rose, why is you mother joining my father on stage?" Asha whispered. Lady Marza had not participated in the battle, of course, but joined them on their journey to the capital, and had rejoined them after the mêlée was done, and had been helping tend to the wounded.

"What, my mother? I have not the faintest idea!" Rose whispered back.

But immediately Asha knew. It made too much sense.

How had she never wondered before that Rose has always been given the exact same education that she had. That the expectations for Rose were always equal to the level that she was required to perform. The bar was set tremendously high for both of them.

Rose had never been treated as a servant or as staff. Maybe because Rose was a year older and Asha looked up to her, Asha had never questioned any of this, but she'd known that Rose had very few actual Lady-in-Waiting responsibilities. Asha gasped and squeezed Rose's hand tightly.

Asha looked at her friend with wide, emotional eyes. "What is it?" Rose asked, but before Asha could answer Lady Marza began to speak.

"Wonderful people of Marian, Zanzia, and Nadroj. I am not one of you. This is indeed my first time in Zanzia. I have, however, spent some time in Nadroj."

"What does she mean she has been to Nadroj?" Rose whispered to Asha, "She never told me that!"

Rose's mother went on. "It is a beautiful land that I loved very much. Fifteen years ago, a delegation from Pome went to meet with King Dokar in an attempt to negotiate, and I was part of that delegation. The negotiations went poorly, but during that time I met Constantine, and we fell in love.

We married in secret, during my visit, with the blessings of the Queen of Pome. I wanted to stay with him in Nadroj, but he thought it was too dangerous for us at the time. He sent me back to Pome so I would be safe. He was to join me the following month, once he had his affairs in order. He never arrived."

Lady Marza turned from the crowd to speak directly to Rose, who was squeezing Asha's hand so much it hurt. "I have always told my daughter that her father died before she was born, and this was true. She just always assumed that her father was my first husband. The father to her sisters. But in truth, she comes from Royal Nadroji blood. She looked very different from her sisters, and even when she was quite young, people began to ask questions. In order to keep her identity a secret, I sent her here, to Zanzia, to be raised in safety. It will come as a much greater surprise to her than to all of you, but it is my great honor to present the next Queen of Nadroj, my daughter, and the daughter to Constantine, Queen Rose."

Rose made a sound next to Asha that sounded like the strangulation of a bird. Asha knew that this moment must be tremendously shocking for her dearest friend. But she also knew that Nadroj could be in no better hands. She embraced Rose (who seemed ready to faint). She said quietly, but firmly, into Rose's ear: "You will make an even better queen than I. The future is in good hands my dear friend."

In a much louder voice Asha yelled, "Long live Queen Rose!"

Thousands of voices chorused back to her: "LONG LIVE QUEEN ROSE!" as Rose walked shakily to join her mother and King Henrick.

The crowd refused to go silent, and there was nothing more to say, so Rose just stood there, taking it all in. She motioned for Asha and Aurelia to join her, the crowd pushing them forward. The three girls stood together, took each other's hands, and raised them into the air. They were three queens to be, and the crowd roared its approval.

The three girls, Rose, Asha, and Aurelia looked at each other and each shared the same thought. In the weeks and years ahead they would all become queens of contiguous kingdoms. They would negotiate with each other and rely on each other to enforce treaties and allow trade. They would be fair and kind and good to their people and their neighbors. They would dispel violence and make sure their youth were educated. They would become architects of vibrant economies.

The world was how it should be.

EPILOGUE

To ensure that no power vacuum in Nadroj would take place now that King Dokar was imprisoned, Rose was immediately sent on her way to rightfully claim her place on the Nadroji throne as its Queen. Asha desperately wanted to go with her, but she was consumed with the responsibilities of uniting two nations, Zanzia and New Marian. She would be there for Rose's coronation set for one month from that day.

But Rose did not travel to the north alone.

Max and his wife Martha insisted on escorting Rose to Nadroj. They had children and grandchildren they were missing, and were eager to finally go home after all these years. Rose was relieved and delighted to have her childhood mentor joining her. The group continued to grow.

The captain of the Nadroji guard, Matias, who had been captured during the fight, pledged his undying loyalty to Rose. He explained that his wife was pregnant with twins, he had three other small children already, and he was needed back home to support his family. In exchange for the favor of letting him return home, Matias would make sure the Nadroji Royal Court accepted Rose and helped her cast out those who would not. Rose decided to trust him.

Together they selected more Nadroji to act as the Queen's Guard. The entire Nadroj army had been on hand to witness the spectacle of Asha defeating King Dokar in that first sword fight so long ago. And they had all been charmed by the fiery redhead who stood unflinching by Asha's side with her bow and arrow cocked at the start of the encounter. They also remembered Rose taking charge of the negotiation process and drafting the terms of the duel, much to the advantage of Zanzia. Though not all of the men, more than enough were eager to accept her as their sovereign. Rose was pleased with the group that she and Matias selected to be the queen's guard.

Rose's mother, Lady Marza, accompanied them north as well, sending for Rose's sisters to join them. An ambassador from the Marians was also selected to join.

In the weeks to come Asha was delightfully entertained by Rose's letters. Rose's mother and sisters took over the castle with gusto. Entire sections of the castle that had been closed for decades, since the time of good King Nret, needed to be reopened before the coronation, according to Lady Marza.

She hired servants and cooks and maids and ladies in-waiting for the castle. They cleaned, and fussed, and ordered new linens, and beds, and cheerful décor.

Rose was on one hand quite glad that she did not have to worry about figuring out any of these details. On the other hand, she wanted to be as far away as possible from the all-encompassing flurry of activity inside the castle.

In an excellent speech that Rose gave to her new people, she ended with the following:

"Good people of Nadroj. I am aware that some of you have concerns about me. You think I am too young. That I am not sufficiently Nadroji. You think I am not cunning or strategic enough. You think I am not tough enough or skilled enough to lead you. But you are wrong, and I will prove myself to you. I am going to give each of you an opportunity to try and prove that you are superior to me. You can challenge me in four areas: sword fighting, Nadroji history and geography, archery, and chess. If any Nadroji can best me in all four duels, I will concede that I am not worthy, and I will not ascend to the throne!"

Asha read this letter aloud to Magnus, who grew immediately very concerned.

"That is madness, Asha! What is she thinking, exposing her right to the throne like that? What if Commander Blackwell takes her on? What if she loses? That would be very bad for the Marians and the Zanzians! I get that she is being very brave and trying to win over her people, but it is a very risky move."

Asha laughed at his concerns and responded first with a smile that said everything would be alright.

"You are actually wrong about this, Magnus. But only because you are still getting to know Rose. The risk is very low. Remember, Rose and I have pretty much been doing three things for most of the last decade. Sword fighting under a master, learning everything there is to know about Nadroj so that I would have a better chance at somehow beating King Dokar, and playing chess for fun. I'm better than Rose at sword fighting, but she is really really good. And there is no one better in all three kingdoms than Rose at archery. Even if she was to lose the sword fight, the Nadroj trivia, and the chess match – all of which are very unlikely, she won't lose at archery. No, this is really all just a ploy to get away from her mother!" Asha said laughing.

While they all adored Lady Marza, she was indeed a bit much.

Whatever the real reasons for Rose's proclamation, the entire kingdom became riveted by the duels. Rose accepted one competitor per day. Thousands of Nadroji traveled to the capital to watch their soon-to-be queen take on seasoned generals, Dokar's former strategists, and general naysayers, (but not Commander Blackwell, who had vanished just before Rose's arrival at the castle). Since Rose and Asha had done these sorts of demonstrations with each other in front of the Zanzians for years, Rose was right at home. While she did not win every match element, she was never bested in all four, and never beaten soundly in any.

While in the beginning the crowds were silent, curious and watchful, as the days wore on the assemblage found themselves more and more cheering for the 14-year-old heiress to the throne. They were astounded by her incredible knowledge of Nadroj itself, delighted by her skill with the sword, entertained by her ability at chess. But as Asha had said, no one could beat her at archery. Watching Rose let arrows fly was like watching magic.

Even if Rose had used the duels as a ploy to take a break from her mother's frantic transformation of the castle, the end result was something that no one could have imagined.

Every time Rose bested another rival in front of the masses, the more the Nadrojians fell in love with the daughter of Constantine, granddaughter to the beloved King Nret.

Every time she named an obscure mountain peak or a long-forgotten prince, every time she clashed swords with a man twice her size or put a self-proclaimed chess master in check mate, every time she drew an arrow certain to hit its intended mark, the Nadrojis fell more in love with their queen.

Meanwhile, back in Zanzia, Asha was busy helping her kingdom get back on its feet. In the first weeks the Marians remained in Zanzia to assist in bringing the once great nation out of poverty and back to its days of glory. Supplies were brought in through the newly opened trade routes. With tools and materials in hand, the Marians descended on the broken Zanzian farms in mass, or as one Zanzian farmer described it, like a reverse locus.

Carpenters and botanists and glaziers and roofers made beautiful restorations, while others repaired fences, tore out weeds, built sheds, and dug trenches for plumbing. Within a very short amount of time decades of neglect were replaced with handsome looking homes and tidy acres of planted crops. The schools and hospitals, and even the castle received the same treatment. The Marians spared no expense. They brought in all the best medical equipment from around the globe and trained the local doctors on how to use them. Every student got a new desk and new textbooks and new paper and pencils. Schoolhouses were expanded so children no longer had to be stuffed into overflowing classrooms.

The coarse burlap clothing that the Zanzians had resigned themselves to were replaced by modern clothes from around the world.

Roads were built by crews of all three nations. No sooner had the road been completed to the coast than the Marians set about procuring a vessel that could be used as a ferry to travel to the island gifted to the Marians by Asha. They created a seafaring transportation system that was free to all to further boost the economy, and this meant that all sorts of fresh delicacies and unique items found their way into Zanzia.

A shipyard sprouted up in the ocean village of Ketch, to build fishing boats. Young Zanzians delightedly left the mountains to try out a different kind of farming, on the sea. A kelp, halibut, and salted salmon roe specialty, once a typical birthday meal in Zanzia, would once again be part of every celebration.

But Asha's favorite items were the books that came in with every convoy.

Plans were drawn up for New Marian. There would be a castle, a series of communities, shared farmland, parks, and a population of ever-growing numbers who would make a home for themselves in their own land between Nadroj and Zanzia. No expense would be spared, as the ancient diamonds continued to support overflowing bank accounts across the world.

Magnus was overseeing the community planning process, with Asha providing critical information about geography, soils, hydrology, and growing seasons in the higher altitudes.

She loved it all and reveled in her good fortune. Her favorite part was at the end of the day. No matter where they were, in Zanzia, New Marian, or under an open sky camping in her precious wild Zanzian fields on the way to New Marian, she and Magnus would find each other, play a game of chess, and then read to each other by firelight from one of the new books that had arrived with all the other supplies from far off lands.

She smiled at him. Asha had resigned herself to an exiled broken life, far from friends and family and Zanzia. He grinned back, curls falling into his dark eyes.

"What are you thinking?" he asked her.

Asha smiled. "That it seems like the mapmaker's mistake worked out for the best after all."

CHARACTER NAMES BY KINGDOM

Kingdom of Zanzia

Alba – the capital city

Asha (Meliasha Esmerelda DeBurn) alias Claire

King Henrick

Queen Kirsten

Aurelia (alias Freyja)

Orrin

Ben

Rose (alias Daisy)

Max Brintmore

Martha Brintmore

Caspian

Dean

Sam

Gregor

Donovan and Victor (the Thomas twins)

Sam

Alec, the animal minder at the castle

Pigeons: Hugo, Esmerelda

Kingdom of Pome

Queen of Pome

Lady Marza (Rose's mom)

Duchess of Cantoon

Padua Mountains

Marcus

Grace, Rose's oldest sister

Kingdom of Celze

Rowan Overbrook - bookbinder from Celze

Kingdom of Dumas

M/V Intrepid

Marian Kingdom

Constable Sven

King Adrien

Queen Takeisha

Benedict

Eustace

Magnus

Kingdom of Nadroj

King Dokar

Major Hammond

King Nret

Lady Mary (Nret's sister)

Constantine (Nret's brother)

Commander Blackwell

Matias – Captain of the queen's guard

ABOUT THE AUTHOR

Meilani Schijvens lives in Juneau Alaska. Mapmaker's Mistake is her first work of fiction. Meilani is the owner of Rain Coast Data, a research and economic consulting firm, and has authored hundreds of economic publications. Her work has been cited by several national publications, including the New York Times and the Washington Post. She is also the owner of Rain Coast Fables. She previously taught Alaska Natural Resource History at the University of Oregon, served as a staffer to the US Legislative Minority Leader in Washington DC, and worked at the Greens Creek Mine. She has a Master of Science from the University of Oregon and a Bachelor of Arts in history from Colby College. Some random facts about the author include that she once lunched with James Michener every day, and she proposed to her husband in Vietnam after knowing him for 9 days. They have two teenage sons.

Discover more at www.mapmakersmistake.com

ACKNOWLEDGMENTS

Thanks to Glen Fairchild for his gorgeous cover illustration, and to Kirsten Shelton for her beautiful chapter heading drawings. Thanks to Charles Westmoreland, for editing this book. I very much appreciate his enthusiasm in helping carry me across the finish line. Thanks to my early readers: Especially my husband Sander Schijvens, who read it on airplanes during business trips, when the monotony of travel was still a part of our lives.

Thanks to Kathy Ruddy, who insisted on reading an unfinished version. "Somehow the randomness of the mistake is getting to me," she wrote. "Maybe it is a larger question -- is the universe Chaos that cannot be solved, just temporarily lived, or Understandable, where our heroes are capable of figuring things out? I like the latter choice." Her wisdom continues to guide me despite her recent passing.

Thanks to Micaela Fowler for reading an early version mostly in the steam room, back in the days where gyms were still gathering places. Thanks to my boys, Zayden and Denali, who had me read it to them aloud (just like the old days) during a long weekend boating in Tracy Arm. They tore apart the dialogue of characters who were the same age as they, improving the book immensely. Thanks also to all of my other friends, especially Eldri, Myra, Julie, and Kathryn for supporting me in my crazy dream to write this story.

Made in the USA
Las Vegas, NV
23 November 2021